Amber Knows Best

Jo Stewart

With a foreward by

Thomas Wayne King

Copyright © 2015 Jo Stewart

All rights reserved.

ISBN-13: 978-1517625740

Front & back cover image and design, Copyright © 2015 Chuck Shingledecker
www.chuckshingledecker.com

Back cover headshot, Copyright © 2011 Anna Martineau Merritt

Acknowledgements

Special thanks to the St. Croix Writers group for their weekly encouragement and inspiration, to Agnes Kennard and Jackie Dodson for their editing. To Anna Martineau Merritt for the beautiful portrait of mom. To Chuck Shingledecker for helping to organize the publication of the book, and to Dr. Tom King for writing the forward. Also, thank you to Amber, mom's beloved furry companion, who had a special spot in her heart as she wrote this book. – *Kay (Stewart) Lavey*

AMBER KNOWS BEST

Foreword

Cozy Cove is where it all happened. A modest lakeside log cabin, nestled in dense cedar forest overlooking a small bay of Upper St. Croix Lake, became a shared creative center, shaping lives in our own family, this village, and northwestern Wisconsin.

At age 80, my grandfather, Ernest Favell, built this little cabin in 1950. He lived, painted, and wrote there for the remainder of his long life. Cozy Cove became our family Northland adventure base for years.

Even then, as a young teenager, I knew the next fortunate owners of Cozy Cove would have to be kind, remarkable people. They were. We had met the Stewarts.

Jim and Jo Stewart became the new, caring stewards of sunlit Cozy Cove in 1964. With the help of their growing family, Jim and Jo rebuilt, expanded and loved their quiet haven for five decades. During her 50 years there, Jo thrived in a creative, exuberant life centered on their peaceful headwaters home. She shared her joy and considerable talents with all of us who knew her as mentor, actor, teacher, comedian, neighbor, author, friend.

Amber Knows Best was born in Jo's literate Cozy Cove thoughts around 2003. Husband Jim had passed on. Jo's companion became abundant, productive solitude livened by visits from her grown children with their families, her numerous good friends, and her house cats...especially Amber.

Jo created and wrote prolifically across multiple topics over her years alone.

With Amber as her present friend and muse, Jo's essays and stories flowed and were published in media nationwide. CNN featured her often outrageous Thursday morning laughing group, and Jo was a founding member of St. Croix Writers'. Both became cherished, lasting cultural contributions to the Northland.

Eventually, Jo wove dear Amber into a fictional romantic tale of lakeside living in this vibrant yet delicate Upper St. Croix watershed. In her book, Jo preserved regional observations and details, shared her emotions of past years, and left a memorable, glowing story of days and dreams at Cozy Cove.

As you enjoy Amber Knows Best, please think of Jo and her rich creative years with her cats, family, and those so fortunate to be among her friends and loved ones. My wife, our sons and I are forever changed because we knew Jo Stewart. We know our sentiments are echoed by all whose lives she touched.

Amber Knows Best will delight and acquaint you with Amber the perceptive cat and her discerning wisdom...and with Cozy Cove, where it all happened.

– Thomas Wayne King

Chapter One

The drone of an old outboard heading north, and the dark clouds building to the south, were sure signs rain was coming. A heron slowly winged its way south over the choppy waters looking for better fishing nearer the river. Neither man nor bird could see the short, plump woman fishing from the beached wooden raft partially hidden in the cove.

Still, Kate knew she was being watched. From the cabin's screened porch fifty feet up the wooded hillside, a chunky cream-colored Tomcat with amber eyes was observing the scene below. Together they eyed a red and white bobber nestled in the lily pads. Intermittent raindrops poked bubbles in the cove's still surface. The bobber began to move.

"I think we got one, Amber," Kate said, rising awkwardly to her feet. The cat started pacing on the porch floor, purring in anticipation of a meal forthcoming. The rod bent slightly with the weight of her catch as she lifted a large, wiggling panfish out of the water.

"It's a nice one, Amber." Kate held the fish high so her cat could see. "And it didn't even take the worm!" Rain peppered Kate's face as she looked up toward the house. A hanging bird feeder partially obscuring her view was a grim reminder of a job she couldn't do alone.

As she deftly lowered the large bluegill into the live bag, the rain increased its intensity, accompanied by a loud rumble of thunder in the distance. She collected the fishing gear and headed up the maze of boardwalks and steps leading to the house. When she approached the first landing, a long-haired, white-legged kitty appeared from under the deck, cautiously sniffing the flopping catch.

"Hi, Boots. Where have you been? I could have used your help fishing today."

By the time they reached the garage, both Kate and her feline companion were waterlogged from the drops, turned downpour. Neither noticed the small, compact car as it pulled up behind them. The horn's blare sent Boots, and two other cats that had emerged from the cluttered workbench, scurrying in a frightened panic. Kate's momentary alarm melted when she heard the familiar shriek of her boisterous friend, Kerrie Wagner.

"Kate Stenson, I thought you were dead!"

Amused, Kate turned to observe Kerrie's tan, sleek figure explode from the car. She wrapped herself around Kate's dripping form and continued her tirade.

"Larry and I have been up at the cabin for a week. Don't you answer your phone? I wrote I was coming today. Don't they deliver mail in Lake Crystal after Labor Day? I suppose you've been sitting on that blasted dock for the last two months."

Kerrie's high-energy monologue pelted Kate's numb body. The two women were a study in contrasts. Ever since Kate and Kerrie became neighbors thirty years ago in Middleton, Wisconsin--a city one hundred miles south of Lake Crystal--Kerrie's managerial skills had blossomed.

It became a routine back then, when there were more children than pets in their respective households, after the kids were sent off to school, and Kerrie had her life and house in order, she would--promptly at 9:30--march next door into Kate's anything but tidy kitchen to help Kate organize her life. Most of the time Kerrie had already thought out the perfect solution to either the world's or Kate's pressing problems.

Today was no different.

"Quick, get in the house and change your clothes. We're going out to eat," Kerrie said, as she pushed Kate through the cluttered garage. At the doorway to the kitchen, the usually unstoppable Kerrie screeched to a halt. "My Gosh, Kate, what's this?" Distastefully, Kerrie nudged a tin tray of food with her brightly polished toenail. "Are you still running an animal shelter? You've already got an inside cat. I thought you were going to get rid of the Outsiders after Reed died."

Again, answering her own questions, she followed Kate, who hadn't stopped, but just kept plodding through the door ahead of her nervous friend. "I know, Dr. Doolittle, you like talking to the animals."

Suddenly Kerrie grabbed the tail of Kate's bedraggled fishing shirt.

"Wait a minute, Madam. Are you actually bringing that fish into the house to clean?"

"Why not?" Kate dropped the live bag into the sink.

"Why not?" Kerrie nearly screamed in disbelief. "Because they smell, and it's not sanitary. I made Larry build a fish-cleaning room at our cabin...sink and everything. I just got sick and tired of picking fish scales off my kitchen counter top, house plants, everywhere I looked."

Kate unsheathed the fillet knife and pointed it at Kerrie. "If I had a husband..." Kerrie saw the hurt in her friend's eyes.

"I'm sorry, sweetie," she said. Quickly changing the subject, she volunteered, "I'll start your bath water while you do the fish." Her raspy voice faded as she headed down the hall.

With a practiced hand, Kate filleted the fish. Amber, who had streaked downstairs at the sound of Kerrie's voice, reappeared just as suddenly to oversee the cleaning process.

"Sorry, Amber. None for you this time." Kate removed a container half-filled with frozen fish, laid the fresh fillets on top, added water, and popped the container back in the freezer just as Kerrie returned from her mission.

"Your bawth is drawn, Milady," she mimicked. "What does Milady choose to wear?"

Before Kate could stop her, Kerrie about-faced and bee-lined for Kate's bedroom. Grimacing at the unmade bed, she swiftly opened the closet bi-fold door. Two shoes and four sweaters fell down from the top shelf. Kerrie shook her head, and Kate knew why.

Kicking aside what had fallen, Kerrie sorted through the hanging garments and pulled out a slightly wrinkled pair of blue slacks. Still in her British valet mode she quipped, "It's a bit nippy out today, so Milady will need some leg cover and something for the arms."

Suddenly dropping her domestic act, she turned, blouse in hand. "Kate, what size is this?" Again answering herself, she read the label, "Extra large. Well, it looks like a maternity top." With a quick nod toward the bathroom,

Kerrie directed: "Come with me, child. We've got to talk."

Over the years Kate had come to know what that really meant. Kerrie talked, Kate listened. In this case, Kate soaked and Kerrie lectured. "I'm really serious, Kate. I've kept quiet long enough. You've dropped out of the world."

Kerrie rattled on and on, and Kate in her hot water stupor barely heard about how her life had gone to pot and her house, clothes, and BODY reflected it. "It just isn't healthy. And speaking of health," Kerrie said, "When was the last time you were in for a check-up, Kate?"

* * *

Later that evening, after Kerrie had dragged Kate through the process of going out for pie and coffee, and finally departed, Kate had HER say. Reaching down to stroke Amber's soft silky hair, she talked and her feline companion listened.

"Kerrie wasn't right about everything you know."

Amber purred in agreement, and jumped up on the newspaper-strewn sofa beside his mistress.

"I still keep myself busy. I haven't dropped out of life...completely." She looked up at the cobweb dangling from the dining room hanging lamp---chained from the high A-frame wood beam that she and Reed had laughed themselves silly over varnishing. "Maybe I have let the house go a bit, but I'm healthy," she said, reassuring herself.

"Come on, cat, it's getting late." With some difficulty she scooped up Amber's chunky body. "Say, boy, you're putting on weight. How long has it been since YOUR last check-up?"

Walking toward the bedroom, she paused by the *Things to Do* reminder pad posted on the refrigerator. Struggling to shift her lead-heavy cat to one hand, Kate printed in large letters "Call the Vet." She put the pencil in place, took several steps toward the bedroom, and then, as an after thought, turned back to the reminder pad and added, "Call the Clinic".

Climbing into bed, she plunked her pet next to the pillow where Ree used to sleep. Looking into Amber's large yellow eyes, she half smiled. "Amber, we're just a couple of happy fat cats." Then her smile dimmed. "Well, we're fat anyway."

AMBER KNOWS BEST

Chapter Two

Kate's fingers trembled as she buttoned her blouse. "What is there about this trip to the doctor that has you so rattled?" Kate asked herself. "You'd think you were meeting Ben Gessler for the first time." She smiled as she remembered what a stir Ben's appearance had caused back then.

Dr. Gessler had joined the Northview Clinic as a youngster fresh out of medical school the same year Kate, Reed, and their two children decided to move to northern Wisconsin and make the cabin their permanent home. Known as the "Hippie Doctor," he shocked the town with his shoulder length red hair and single earring. Kate chuckled now as she recalled the story that went the rounds about Joe Briggs' first encounter with Ben.

"I don't want that 'Hippie Doctor' working on me!" Joe had screamed when they wheeled him into emergency, bleeding profusely from a pulping accident. As luck would have it, the *Hippie* was the only doctor working that shift.

Fortunately, the painkillers did their job before Ben arrived, so Ben and Joe never really met face to face until 48 hours later. By then it was common knowledge that Joe would live to cut pulp again only because that young Hippie had used his considerable medical skills and stayed by Joe's side until he was out of shock and into intensive care. Joe left the hospital a convert.

A knock on the door brought Kate abruptly back to the present. She gave a final yank to her panty hose, which placed the elastic waist only halfway over her ample hips.

"Mrs. Stenson?" Shelby, Dr. Gessler's young nurse, poked her head around the door. "When you're dressed, the doctor would like to see you in his office."

Kate looked startled, then concerned. "Talk to me! I thought he said everything looked good?"

Shelby smiled and shook her head. "Oh, don't worry. He probably only wants to set up a couple of tests. Just routine stuff. It has been awhile since your last visit, you know." Kate was relieved, but the strange, uneasy feeling didn't go away.

Dr. Gessler stood quickly when Kate entered the small office, offering her a chair opposite his cluttered desk. The fluttery, sinking feeling increased as Kate sat down and Ben walked around to her side. "How are things going, Kate?"

When she thought about it later, she couldn't recall the exact sequence of events, nor really why it happened. She did remember the question. It was one she had been asked a trillion times over the past year, but this time her reaction was completely out of character.

Maybe it was his pale blue eyes that seemed to look deep into her heart. Maybe it was the touch of his warm hand on hers. She opened her mouth for the ritual answer, but instead, somewhere from within the depth of her soul came a low moan, followed by dry sobs that cranked open a water valve that had been clamped shut for years.

Kate never cried in public. Not when her mother died two years ago, nor when Reed died a year later. Her family counted on her being a tower of strength in a crisis.

She certainly wasn't a tower of strength now. The tower had been felled by a downpour of unspent tears that seemed to ebb and flow in unquenchable waves of misery.

When Kate finally pulled herself up out of the dark hole of grief, and became aware of the world around her, she noticed Dr. Gessler was still holding her hand, and there was a giant box of Kleenex in her lap. Kate grabbed a generous amount and blew her nose – vaudeville style. She quickly decided the best thing to do under the circumstances was just pretend that the preceding display of emotion had never happened. Stiffening her spine while straightening her tear-soaked blouse, Kate looked straight into Ben's eyes and lifted her chin regally. "How are things going, you asked?" She cocked her head, pasted a crooked smile on her face and quipped with artificially perfect diction, "Just fine, thank you."

For a moment time froze. Neither spoke. Kate didn't because she had given the cue, and felt the next line was his. Ben didn't, maybe because her unexpected acting skills had done what Kate hoped, effectively changed the mood.

What followed wasn't scripted either. Ben started to laugh. It started as a deep, infectious chuckle, and progressed to a full-blown roar. Kate, who hadn't had a good laugh in two years, felt herself being drawn into his mirth. When their laughter subsided, Ben's next question caught Kate off guard, "Ever keep a diary when you were a teen?"

"Why? I thought all young girls kept a diary. In my case there was no point in it. I always told my mother everything I did."

"Oh? But did you tell your mother how you FELT about what you did?"

"Of course!" She replied indignantly.

"Of course!" Ben mimicked with a look that said otherwise. "Kate, I want you to do something for me. No, I want you to do something for YOURSELF. For the next week I want you to keep a daily journal. This is not a chronicle of events, it's your reactions or feelings about those events."

Kate shook her head. "I'm afraid my life is not too eventful these days."

"Oh, I don't necessarily mean big events. Even a phone conversation might trigger feelings. I gather you told your mother what she wanted to hear, but your real feelings might have surprised her."

That evoked a chuckle from Kate, but no comment. She eyed her doctor suspiciously, "Are you going to be reading this?"

"Nope...well, there is one part I would like to see, but you can keep it separate. I'd also like you to keep a daily log of what you eat and when you eat it. That's everything now, snacks included." From Ben's desk drawer he fished out two notebooks. He also handed Kate a slip of paper. "These are a couple of test dates to keep. And one final thing. I asked Shelby to copy down your weight chart since you've been coming to the clinic. There is a pattern here, but I can't figure it out. If you like mysteries, maybe you can unravel this one."

As Ben opened the office door, he smiled and winked mischievously. "Remember the two "F's"–feelings and food. I've made an appointment for next week...same time...same station. Have fun investigating, Nancy Drew."

AMBER KNOWS BEST

Chapter Three

"Amber, get your furry face out of my cereal dish. You know cream isn't on your diet. And maybe it shouldn't be on mine," Kate said, as she looked over the dates and weights listed on the paper Dr. Gessler gave her yesterday.

It was then she remembered her promise, flipped open the small notebook, and began listing her breakfast bill-of-fare.

Day 1 Breakfast   8:30 a.m.

1 small glass frozen orange juice

1 large bowl of shredded wheat topped with raspberries

½ cup half and half

2 pieces of buttered whole wheat toast

1 tsp apricot preserves

2 cups of coffee (black)

Just writing the menu stimulated Kate's appetite again. She changed line four to read three pieces of toast, and headed for the breadbox. As she passed the wide expanse of windows facing the lake, she noticed some unfamiliar movement several feet from the neighbor's dock. Grabbing her binoculars, she quickly identified three otter heads and tails bobbing in the waves. A great blue heron stood motionless on the nearby boat ramp, silently observing the aquatic trio.

Kate knew why the otter had returned. Her neighbors, the Hellmans, were in the process of selling their Lake Crystal Lodge acreage, so the main log house and guest cabin stood empty. Kate smiled and thought – less human activity means more undisturbed time for the native wild life...and me. One of the otters lumbered onto the boat ramp banked against the shore, slid across the wet boards, and dove into the water again.

For some reason, the memory of Kerrie's last visit pulled Kate away from the window. Kerrie's accusations hounded her as she plopped the bread into the toaster. "You know, Kate, you're fast becoming a recluse…a hermit. Tell me, who's your best friend these days…your cat, Amber?" Kate spread the warm toast with a generous topping of butter and apricot preserves, then returned to the table. Amber hadn't moved far from the cereal bowl.

"Amber, I'd be honored to have you as my best friend. You satisfy all the requirements. You're there when I need you. You accept me…warts and all. We have lots in common. We are bird watchers and home bodies." Kate took a large bite of toast and pushed the cereal dish close enough for Amber to lick the few drops of cream remaining. "And you like to eat as much as I do. What more do we need?" For some reason, that last question rang a little hollow to Kate's ears, so she continued on firmer ground.

"Today is YOUR day to see the doctor." Amber lifted his head from the cereal dish and eyed Kate with suspicion. "But you're luckier than I am. Your doctor makes house calls. You are also luckier than I am because I'm sure Dr. Scheer won't give you an assignment like I got."

Kate reflected that "assignment" wasn't exactly the word Ben Gessler had used, but she certainly felt like a kid in school when she opened the large, red, spiral notebook and stared at the blank page. With a sigh of resignation, she printed the heading in bold strokes:

Day 1

Dear Diary Ben,

I just thought of another reason why I never kept a diary. I don't like telling my feelings to a BOOK. It's like talking to a toadstool or a chair.

I know you won't be reading this, Ben, but I hope your ears twitch and your fingers burn every time I have to put my FEELINGS down on paper. I don't know whether you noticed yesterday, but I don't handle feelings real well. Although I must admit after my outburst in your office, I slept better last night than I have for quite a while.

I know you meant well, and I know my friend Kerrie means well, but somehow I get the impression I should be all perky and happy now. Kerrie's words were "I've left you alone for a year now"–like something happens on the 13th month? All the hurt goes away – poof!

And another thing. Did you think looking at my weight gain over the years was going to lift my spirits? I haven't figured out the mystery yet, but I'm working on it. I've started charting on some graph paper the weight gain with the events in my life. Right now the chart looks like a very successful United Way Campaign. Yesterday's weight figure put us way over the top.

The slam of a car door sent Amber off the table and Kate to the entranceway to wait for one of her favorite visitors, Dr. Joanne Scheer. Kate held the outside door open. The doctor scraped mud from her laced leather high-tops onto the welcome mat before she came in the warming room.

"My first stop was a barn visit to check on a pet lamb that was under the weather," she explained with a ready smile. "And speaking of barn pets, I saw Blackie and Boots on my way through the garage, but I didn't see Twin," Dr. Scheer said, and followed Kate into the living room.

Kate shook her head. "Twin's still the skittish one, doggone it. Of the four Outsiders, that tiny little tiger is my favorite. She'll be around for love and food before long, I hope."

Dr. Scheer asked, "Where's Amber?"

Suddenly Kate realized that in her intent to put her feelings on paper for Ben, she had forgotten to close all her pet's escape routes. Amber was always suspicious of strangers and infrequent visitors.

"I'll help you locate him," the doctor volunteered. "I remember some of his hide-outs.

The search was a short one. The closet downstairs under the stairwell was Amber's favorite retreat, so Kate looked there first. Dr. Scheer quickly prepared the immunizations, and so slickly administered the shots, Amber barely stirred in Kate's arms. She talked to Amber throughout the examining process, telling him how beautifully he kept his cream coat, and what striking amber eyes he had.

"He'll be pretty hard to live with hearing all that blarney," Kate protested as she watched the doctor put away the stethoscope and document Amber's medical file. "So Amber is in good shape?"

"Yep! Lookin' good, except for one thing." Dr. Scheer lifted Amber out of Kate's arms. "Whoa! Just as I thought. Amber, you are beautiful, but you are also much heavier than my last visit." She handed the docile cat back to Kate with a loving pat. The phone interrupted their conversation.

"I'll get it if I may," the doctor said. "I gave your number to my next appointment."

"Would you like some coffee?" Kate asked. Dr. Scheer smiled her approval, and Kate transferred a couple of doughnuts from the freezer to the microwave. She also conscientiously added, "1 doughnut" to her Day 1 food log.

"This is one of the perks of my job." Dr. Scheer's blue eyes sparkled as she dunked a large cake doughnut into her coffee mug.

"It certainly doesn't show on you," Kate said, silently comparing the doctor's petite slender shape to her own.

"I don't sit still long enough for it to do much harm." Her eyes rested on Amber, who was watching Kate return the milk to the refrigerator.

"Back to Amber's weight problem. I have some diet cat food we can try. I trust you're not giving him table food?"

"Amber? Join me at the table?" Kate's voice registered exaggerated horror.

Dr. Scheer chuckled. "I'd start by mixing Amber's regular food with diet food, then just hope for the best."

Kate looked confused, "Why do you say that?"

"If Amber finds the food palatable we're in luck. If he doesn't, we'll have to try something else. Cats are the only animals I know who will starve rather than eat what they don't like." Kate moved over to the back of the love seat where Amber had draped himself. She stroked him under the chin, looking into his half-closed eyes. "If he won't eat the diet food, isn't there something else I can do?"

"Oh, sure there is. You can cut back on the quantity of the food he is eating now, and we'll work out an exercise program." Dr. Scheer patted

Kate's shoulder on her way to the door. "I've got some diet food in my van you can try. Don't worry. We'll get Amber back in shape."

Kate followed the doctor to the van and took the bag of cat food she offered. As she watched Dr. Scheer drive away, Kate couldn't decide what was heavier, the bag of food in her left arm, Amber on her right, or her ego, which had been dealt yet another blow.

"Gosh Amber, I'm not even doing a very good job of raising you. What next?"

Kate pushed her head in Amber's fur to blot the tears spilling down her cheeks.

AMBER KNOWS BEST

Chapter Four

Day 2

Dear Ben,

RIDDLE: What has fat cheeks, almost white hair, and an eating problem?

ANSWER: My cat, Amber.

If you guessed me, you're in big trouble, Mister. Although I have to admit there is more than a little resemblance these days. I used to laugh loud and long at those pictures of dog owners who look like their pets. I'm not laughing today. Amber is on his second day of diet cat food, and he hasn't swallowed the first morsel. He is sitting beside his food dish now, giving me a forlorn look that clearly says, "I can't believe you are doing this to me."

While I'm on the subject of food, today I cracked the weight chart mystery. Remember the sheet of paper you gave me with my weight figures over the years I've been coming to the clinic? As I matched my weight gains with events, I found a correlation with the ups and downs in my life. Case-in-point: The summer I went on a dandy European Alpine holiday with my mother and sister, I ate my way through five countries, and in three weeks gained seven pounds. Understandable. Paradoxically, the year of Reed's illness I also gained seven pounds. I'm not sure if your medical journals have a name for it, but I fear I'm one who acts out my feelings at the dinner table. I eat when I'm happy, and I eat when I'm sad. At the rate my life's going, I should be blimp size soon. I'll just float over to your office for my next appointment. I'd rather eat than talk about it, so on to a new subject.

This afternoon I plan to do something to the disorganized mess I lovingly call a home. I've contacted a cleaning person who has her Master's degree in tidiness. In fact, I hear her coming now.

"I'm here, Gramma! Where do we start?"

Kate felt a tingle of joy at the sound of her young granddaughter's voice.

"I'm in the bedroom, Courtney."

Courtney bounded into the room, her blue eyes bright with a "take charge" look. Eagerly, she pulled open the bi-fold door and then shook her head in disbelief.

"This closet is a mess, Gramma! Where shall we start?" A sweater fell off the top shelf and landed briefly on Courtney's head before joining the mish-mash of shoes on the closet floor. Kate's habit of throwing rather than placing items on that shelf had a boomerang effect each time the door opened.

"You're the boss here, Courtney. Just tell me what to do." Kate knew nothing made her six-year-old granddaughter happier than giving orders, a skill she practiced daily on her four-year-old brother, Matthew.

Courtney disappeared briefly, and returned dragging the stepladder Kate kept in the utility room. "Let's start at the top," Courtney suggested. "You put everything off the shelf, on the bed, and I'll put it in stacks the way Momma does it."

While they each worked on their assigned task, Courtney talked about kindergarten.

"You know what my favorite time is? Story time. Oh, I almost forgot to tell you, Gramma. I volunteered you to my teacher yesterday."

"You did what?"

"Mrs. Shannon asked if we knew any good story tellers, so I volunteered you. She asked me to ask you if you'd come tell our class stories next Tuesday. Can you?"

Hoping to put Courtney off, Kate sputtered, "Oh, the kids wouldn't like any of the stories I tell."

"Oh, yes they would! You tell "The Three Billy Goats Gruff" lots better than the teacher reads it. Do that mean ol' Troll for me now, Gramma. Please!"

"We'll never get our job done here, Courtney, if we take time out for play acting." Kate knew what a goal setter her granddaughter was, so she had pulled the right string to get her back on track.

"Ok, Gramma, but I'll be awful disappointed if you can't do it on Tuesday." It struck Kate that Courtney appeared to know what strings to pull as well.

After the top shelf was organized, Courtney surveyed the hanging clothes with some concern.

"Gramma!" she whined in exasperation, "You've got everything all jumbled together."

"I know. Some of these clothes I don't wear anymore."

"Why? Which ones?"

"The slacks. I'll try them on now to see which ones to keep."

So, while Courtney climbed the stepladder and put the short items – blouses and skirts – together in one section, Kate tried on slacks.

After Courtney completed the clothes sorting, she moved on to the closet floor and the pairing of her grandmother's shoes. Meanwhile, Courtney kept an eye on Kate's gyrations as she tried on one pair of slacks after another, putting them on the discard pile when her hips and the pants size didn't match.

Intent on her task, Kate didn't see that Courtney had finished her work and was now sitting on the bed contemplating the ever-growing stack of cast off slacks.

"You know what I think, Gramma?"

"Kate turned to face Courtney with a smile. "What do you think, Courtney?"

"I think you've got a big butt, and you'd better do something about it before it gets any bigger."

* * *

Later that evening Kate talked and Amber listened.

"Amber, I think you have a big belly, and you'd better do something about it before it gets any bigger."

Amber started to walk away, but Kate grabbed him and spoke directly to his face.

"I know this isn't something you want to hear. Quite frankly I felt the same way when similar facts were presented to me earlier today. But I've had some time to think about it, and have made a decision. Granted there are some things we can't change. After all, we are products of our genetics. When you came to live with us as a yearling, you were chunkier than your skinny cousin Casey. Even when I was first married and only weighed 110 pounds, my hips were my biggest asset. But over the past several years we've let things get out of hand. We've gotten fat. When I walked Courtney home this afternoon, I was puffing before I got to the top of our hill. PUFFING! I'm only 60 years old, Amber, and you're nine, which is about the same in cat years. We've got some life ahead of us if we play our health cards right, and by gum, we're going to start living that healthy life style tomorrow!"

As if to punctuate that last remark, Kate gave Amber a kiss on his furry chest, wrote "Tell stories to Kindergarten Class Tuesday" on her calendar, and marched down the hall to her bedroom – like a woman with a mission.

Chapter Five

The early morning September air had a brisk flavor of fall to it as Kate filled the tin tray with cat food. The sound of food pellets brought Blackie and Boots down the ladder one at a time, stretching the kinks out of their stiff legs from their overnight stay in the garage loft.

"Hey you guys, where's your sister? Hm? I suppose she still has a case of wanderlust."

As the cats rubbed their purring bodies against her legs, Kate thought fondly of her husband, Reed, and when these cats came to join the family. Reed was a lover, and that included cats. Two years ago a feral female had delivered a litter of four somewhere on the property, weaned them and then disappeared. The babies were a feisty crew – two males and two females – who managed to fend for themselves until the first heavy snow. The storm came while Kate was 250 miles away visiting their daughter Jill's family. Kate returned to find Reed had improvised a cat shelter on the back deck made out of bundles of newspaper and hay as flooring. The grandchildren's plastic swimming pool served as a roof.

Reed's illness had forced his retirement that fall, so feeding and taming the cats became his project. The males, Blackie and Boots, were amenable to his advances. They even accepted their neutering without much ado. Not so the twins, distinguishable only when together, and so named Twin and Little Twin. They were onto Reed's tricks of sweet talk, followed by his fishnet capture. The girls both got themselves pregnant the following spring, and might have gone full term if their lust for tuna fish hadn't caught them unawares. They ate; Reed grabbed them, and shoved them both into a Pet Carrier for a visit to Dr. Scheer.

That wasn't the end of the story, however. The day both cats were strong enough to be set free, Little Twin left home with nary a backward glance. Kate thought she spotted her near the neighbor's guest house one day, but the distance was too great for positive identification. Her sister, Twin, had evidently been snagged by the warmth of human love. So, denying her feral roots, she stayed until just a week ago, when she, too, disappeared.

Kate stroked the soft, longhaired calico body of Boots with one hand,

and with the other scratched the forehead of his shorthaired brother, Blackie. She stood to look once again for Twin beyond the blue-cushioned lawn chair, and into the woods. As Reed's energy failed him, he'd spent much of each summer day sitting in that chair, surrounded by his three cat friends – Blackie and Boots curled up on his lap, and Twin at his feet.

The memory was interrupted by the sharp jingle of the phone. Once inside, Kate looked at the stove clock with concern. Eight on Saturday morning was too early for a social call. Her fingers trembled on the receiver as she spoke.

"Hello?"

"Is this the Loch Ness Monster?"

Immediately Kate's apprehension vanished. "Kerrie! Where are you?"

"Surprise! We're back at the cabin again, closing up for the season."

"Closing up! Why? Fall is the prettiest time of the year. You never close up this early."

"I know," Kerrie explained. "That is why I'm calling. We barely got home last week when our ever-on-the-move daughter, Donna, called from Phoenix saying she has finally decided to put down roots and buy a home. Naturally she wants our advice on this big step. Len and I may be moving west ourselves now that he's retired."

Kerrie paused and her voice softened. I guess I should have mentioned this a while back. But you know, Kate, all five kids live out there, so why not?"

This unexpected news was a blow. Kate grabbed the back post of the high-back telephone chair and sat down. "Kerrie! Isn't this kind of sudden?"

"I said MAYBE moving. We're renting an apartment in Phoenix for six months to see if we like it."

Kate's voice reflected her disappointment. "Phoenix is so far away." Then her mood changed. "Doggone it, Kerrie. Two months ago I tried to convince you to buy the place next door, but now it's too late. I walked past the gate entrance yesterday and noticed a Sold sign."

Suddenly Kerrie became the Inquiring Reporter. "OK, lady, give me the facts. Who are the new owners, and where are they from?"

Kate laughed at her friend's gossipy nature. "I haven't the faintest. I've never seen anyone even looking at the place." She turned toward the window as she spoke, and became aware of movement. "Hey, wait a minute. Would you believe this? I think I see an old pick-up truck coming up the drive now?"

"Quick! Get your binoculars, Kate, and give me the details."

Kate grabbed her field glasses from the shelf near the window, and felt like a spy as she adjusted the lens. "You're a nut, Kerrie, but here goes. A man is getting out of the truck."

"A man? How old? What does he look like?"

Kate chuckled at Commander Kerrie's style of interrogation. "Hey! We're talking distance here. There's a half a block and a mini- forest of trees between us. But here goes nothing. The gentleman in question has a large frame and looks older. He's wearing what looks like a fishing hat and casual, maybe work clothes. Probably someone hired to get the place in shape before the owners arrive. Oops! He just went in the guesthouse, Sherlock. Sorry I couldn't give you any more details... Say, I got a better idea. Why don't you and Len drive up here for lunch? Then you can case the situation in person."

"I'd love to Kate, but this Phoenix thing came up so quickly, and Donna doesn't want to make the decision without us. As it is, Len and I will have to work like Dutch uncles to close up the cabin and head home before dark. Actually, I've talked longer than I promised, and Len's giving me the high sign to shut up."

They ended their conversation with promises to write and call often. For a while, Kate sat limply, letting the import of Kerrie's news fill her emotional pores. Amber had other plans. With a leap, he jumped from the dining room table to the island counter and then down to his food dish, bringing Kate back to the present. Amber sniffed at the new diet cat food heaped in his dish, then sat down next to this new cuisine--prepared to wait it out. He was on a hunger strike, and like Ghandi, Amber planned to make his point. It would be back to his favorite Cat Chow, or no chow, as far as he was concerned. Kate shook her head. She could sympathize with all of Amber's cat quirks, but some of her friends could not.

"Cats are useless," Kerrie intoned on one of her visits to the Stenson lake home following Reed's death. "What you need now that you're alone, Kate, is a good watch dog chained in your side yard."

For many years, Kerrie's pet of choice was no pet. Her husband, Len, and their kids finally wore down her better judgment and talked Kerrie into George, a black lab. Even then Kerrie issued certain ultimatums. "That dog is to stay outdoors in a dog house, rain or shine, summer and winter. I'll not have dog dirt in my house." Kerrie was true to her word, and George remained an all-weather-all-season, outside pet.

Kate felt sorry for George and his outside status. She grew up in a dog and cat loving family, and that's what those animals all were – members of the family. Reed was partial to cats. He endeared himself to Kate's mother on their first meeting by swapping cat stories. There was, for instance, Old Tom, a Stenson family favorite who had a Milky Way fetish. Old Tom would walk on his hind legs and execute other demeaning tricks for morsels of this chocolate delight.

Kerrie, on the other hand, couldn't find one virtue in the feline family. "A dog," Kerrie pontificated, "could protect you. You can communicate with a dog."

Remembering that conversation, Kate walked over to Amber and sat on the floor beside him. "So, you can't communicate with cats?" Amber's ears perked up, and he put a paw on her lap. In response, Kate scratched between Amber's ears. "I know what that means." Amber purred his thanks. A dog barked in the distance, and Amber's ears swiveled, receptive to every new sound.

"Amber, I can tell what you are thinking just by looking at your ears. Do you remember when that black leopard of a cat jumped at the screened porch door a month ago? You were my protector then. I've never seen you so angry. You flattened your ears back against your head and told that intruder - in a bobcat-like yowl - to get off your turf, and STAY OFF."

Kate put Amber's paws around her neck and held his warm body against hers in a cat hug. "OK, Amber, you've made your point about the diet cat food. But remember, this is the day we start our healthy life style. In the past, my feline friend, you've been eating portions suitable for a St. Bernard." Amber looked up at Kate.

"I know, you're not the only one. I'm not a Sumo wrestler, but I've been eating like one. The point I'm trying to make is, we've been overfilling the tank, and starting now we're going to change."

Kate threw away the pale pellets of diet food and measured ¾ cup of the Cat Chow. Evidently Amber couldn't believe his good fortune. He sniffed at the food and looked back up at Kate. "Oh, it's the real thing all right Amber, but that's your day's ration. So make it last."

Accordingly, Kate reduced her breakfast portions by half, and concluded there was definitely something to be said for the philosophy of diet support groups. She and Amber could commiserate together. Kate also remembered the remedy her mother had for her as a child. Whenever she whined that her stomach ached and she thought she might be sick, her mother would quip, "Just get your mind on something else." So, rather than get out that second slice of bread Kate wanted to eat, she got out her notebook and wrote:

Day 3

Dear Ben,

Any fool can see by looking at my daily food log that I've been eating for two. Since you and I know that is no longer possible, I've decided to start eating meals in proportion to my five feet two frame. I should warn you, however, that in the past, whenever I've cut down on my food rations, I've gotten mean. So be prepared. I've also made a decision about what to do with all the extra non-eating time on my hands. My veterinarian gave me the idea. Yes, I said veterinarian. You're not the only doctor influencing my life, you know.

AMBER KNOWS BEST

Chapter Six

Kate examined her face critically as she dabbed on some powder and lipstick, and decided from the waist up, at least her 60-year-old chassis wasn't too bad. The smooth youthful complexion was a gift from her English father. She had inherited her mother's deep blue green eyes and long dark lashes – limped pools was the cliché Reed liked to use. Those eyes, always reflectors of her mood, radiated frustration. She usually kept her naturally curly, white hair short. Now, with added length, it hung limply around her neck and this morning's attempts to keep the stubborn curls confined in a French twist had failed miserably.

The sound of a hockey game in progress sent Kate to the hallway, where she caught Amber batting a ping pong ball from one baseboard across to the other. On a wild, field goal attempt, the ball whizzed into the living room, banked off the love seat and shot down the stairs, Amber's chunky body in hot pursuit.

Kate smiled. Her plan was working. Dr. Scheer said Amber needed more exercise, so Kate spent time yesterday evening turning the main floor into a feline exercise spa. At this early hour, Amber had already discovered a small basket filled with balls – brightly striped rubber balls, golf balls, and his current favorite – ping pong balls. Another exercise gadget, suspended by an elastic string from the back of the love seat, was a black bodied, red-legged monster called a "Jitter Critter." This creature had the personal recommendation of Dr. Scheer's cat that spent hours trying to kill the beast.

Kate also had exercise in mind for herself. Twin still hadn't returned. So, after breakfast she planned to snoop around over her cat's favorite haunts till she found that wayward lass.

Kate leaned over the deck railing and looked toward the water. Tales of missing children found close to home prompted her to start the search on Twin's home turf. The snap of the back porch screened door had flushed two mallards out of the cover but it didn't hurry the muskrat swimming through the lily pads towards the shore. Kerrie called Kate's home "The Bird's Nest" because of its hill position nestled amongst the tree branches.

Certainly there was plenty to keep cats happily occupied on the Stenson property. They often chased each other – or any other cats in the vicinity –

up to the top most branches of the tall cedars that rimmed the cove. Kate looked out of the tall cedars that rimmed the cove. Kate looked out over the limbs for Twin's darkly striped form. Next, she scanned the four wooden walkways that led steeply down to the lake's edge. The cats often crouched here. Hidden from view by the reeds and cattails, it was easy for them to snare moles, mice, and chipmunks looking for water.

Most of the lake front property owners had tamed the land bordering the water. Not Reed. He had said the incline was too steep and the springs too numerous. So while their neighbors spent hours riding their lawn mowers, Kate and Reed had time to sit on the dock letting the forget-me-nots, jewelweeds, jack in the pulpits, wild raspberries and ferns do the work. Reed called it "conscientious neglect." Kate shared his philosophy.

Fairly satisfied that Twin wasn't hiding at home, Kate walked around the north side of the house, the one level area of her property that she continued to keep in lawn and flowerbeds. On her way, she paused for a moment to admire the brilliant black, red and white plumage of a Pileated Woodpecker circling up the trunk of a large dead birch tree in the adjacent woods. Kate decided to continue her hunt up the west road that bordered the recently sold property.

She reached the top of the hill, then paused by the entrance gate. When the Hellman's were her neighbors, Kate felt free to walk on their land. This time of the year, Matthew and Courtney loved picking up fallen pinecones for their craft projects. Judy Hellman would say, "Bring your grandchildren over this week before we mulch the leaves."

As the gate closed behind her, Kate felt a bit guilty about trespassing now, but her concern over Twin's lengthy disappearance outweighed that legality. At first she stayed close to the split rail fence bordering the road, calling Twin's name softly as she walked. There was one location in particular that she wanted to reach. Reed and Kate used to call it the Evergreen Mall because it was such a popular spot with the cats. From the living room window they could see cat paths leading there all seasons of the year.

The Mall was a thick grove of pine trees. Blue spruce and other lower growing evergreens clustered around the base of two huge Norway Pines. Many times Reed and Kate had wondered aloud why the cats found this spot so attractive, but the grove was so dense that they had never attempted to fight their way into the thicket.

Today was different. Kate had gone this far, so she was determined to go all the way. As she approached the area, she noticed a spot where she could crawl on her hands and knees to a small clearing. Feeling like a kid in a tree fort, Kate sat for a while in the Mall's center calling Twin's name.

Getting no response, Kate started out, this time crawling backwards to protect her face from the branches that were clawing at her sweater and hair. For some reason the path out seemed longer and she became aware of a noise that stopped before she could identify it. Without much advance warning, she was out of the thicket and onto the lawn. As she sat back on her haunches and commenced brushing the twigs out of her hair, she sensed she was not alone.

Looking up, she saw the machine she couldn't identify earlier, a leaf mulcher. Standing behind the mulcher was a tall, broad- shouldered man with close-cropped gray hair and a shocked expression.

Immediately, Kate knew she had some explaining to do. Before she could gather her thoughts, she was being helped, almost lifted to her feet. That action seemed to clear her head and she spoke quickly before her accuser could say anything.

"I'm Mrs. Kate Stenson, and I live next door." She pointed in the general direction of her house. "I'm looking for a lost cat who sometimes wanders over on this property." Kate realized that didn't adequately explain her all-fours exit out of the evergreens, so she continued. "Our cats seem especially attracted to that clump of trees." This time she gestured to the Evergreen Mall. "So I just thought I'd check it out."

Throughout this monologue Kate had carefully averted her eyes from the gentleman in front of her. However, when she reached the end of her rambling, she looked up in helpless defeat. The reaction of her listener was a surprise. In a soft, deep voice, he responded with genuine concern.

"I'm very sorry to hear about your cat, Mrs. Stenson."

Kate felt tears welling up and spilling down her cheeks. She turned away hoping this stranger hadn't noticed/ and quickly continued, "Her name is Twin, and she's a small black and gray tiger with some white on her face, neck and legs. One time the Hellman's dog chased her up a tree, and they lured her down with some canned tuna fish. She can't resist tuna."

"Really? I enjoy tuna myself." As he spoke /Kate turned to see a generous smile transform his tan face and soften his dark eyes. "While I'm working/ I'll certainly keep an eye out for the little lady. I'll let you know if I see her, Mrs. Stenson."

"Thank you Mr. ...." Kate paused.

"Oh forgive me." Taking off his work gloves, he extended his hand. "My name is Paul Dubois." His handshake was warm and firm.

Kate started toward her property and then thought of something. "Oh, Mr. Dubois. Could you tell me when you expect the owners to be moving in?"

She was a distance away from him, and for a moment thought he hadn't heard her. Then he replied, "I expect there will be someone in the main house a week from today."

Waving in response, Kate hurried home.

Day 4

Dear Ben,

Amber and I are exhausted. Today was "Exercise Day," and we may have overdone it. Amber made 10 hockey field goals, that I witnessed, and successfully annihilated his Jitter Critter. I cleaned the whole house and made preparations for my son's birthday dinner tomorrow. Oh, yes. Something else happened. I stumbled, and I mean literally stumbled, on to someone who likes cats. Why should a little thing like that make me feel so good?

Chapter Seven

As Kate ate breakfast, she watched a blue haze of wood smoke drifting toward the lake from the Hellman's main house stone chimney. That was a good indication of a sharp, overnight drop in temperature. Fall could be like that in northwestern Wisconsin – hot as summer one day, and almost cold the next. Paul Dubois was outside already, moving storm windows from the garage to the guesthouse.

Kate had been busy too, setting her agenda for Tuesday. Courtney's teacher, Gail Shannon, had called requesting Kate's presence at the elementary school as storyteller from 1:30 – 2:00, and Shelly, Dr. Gessler's nurse, had called requesting Kate's presence at the Clinic at 2:30.

"That's tomorrow, Amber. Today's my day to play, and I know just what I plan to do. Fish! I've had an itch to fish ever since I watched the fishing activity at Hellman's dock yesterday. At the word fish, Amber's ears perked. Amber trotted behind Kate to the bedroom and jumped on the bed as Kate dressed.

"It's called layering, Amber. That's the trick. So when the temperature warms up, you can take it off." She twirled around in front of the mirror for her pet's benefit. "Of course, in all these extra shirts, I look like Tugboat Annie. But who is going to see me except some hungry panfish – I hope, I hope?"

Boots and Blackie followed Kate down to the beached old raft where the paddleboat was anchored, and watched her load the fishing gear. "I'd like to take you along kids, but I may be awhile."

As Kate pushed off, she positioned the flotation cushion behind her back. Her grandson, Matthew, wasn't the only member of the family with short legs. Her own father stood only five feet five inches. "Small, but mighty fine" was Kate's description of him. While her mother was saying, "Get your mind on something else," her father was providing immediate solutions to her problems.

Kate remembered the year she was ten and was suffering the taunting of her peers," How ya doing, Freckle Face?" She brought her misery to the supper table one summer night, and her father outlined a remedy that had worked for him.

"You must get up before dawn three mornings in a row while the dew is still on the grass. Wet your hands in the dew and rub them over the freckles. Then rub your hands over the area of your body where you want the freckles transferred."

Her father cautioned that it might be the next year before she'd really notice the difference. And of course he was right. By then the freckles had been replaced by pimples, and he had help for those blemishes too.

Kate looked down at the freckles on the back of her hands with a wistful smile. All those strong people who had managed her life--Mother, Dad, Reed, Kerrie--were slowly drifting away–much like her paddleboat was sliding away from the dock, she observed. A ripple in the lily pads close to Hellman's dock could mean fish action. She slowly paddled in that direction and cast out her line.

Paul Dubois was putting the storm windows on the north end of the guesthouse, and waved at her as she moved closer to shore. Here was a puzzle. From their first meeting, Kate felt something about this "handyman" didn't fit. What was it?

A jerk on her line commanded Kate's attention. A fair size fish appeared to have her bait and was moving into the weeds. Kate yanked and felt the hook release. As she reeled in the line, the hook embedded itself in a lily pad and remained secure. Kate prepared to cut the line, then remembered she hadn't brought any extra hooks with her. Aggravated, she paddled over to the area, blindly reached into the weeds, and pulled the lily pad free.

"Yee – ike!" she screeched. The pain of the hook embedded in her finger, brought tears to her eyes. "How much of a fool can you be?" Kate berated herself.

"May I help?" Kate recognized the deep voice of Paul Dubois on the dock, close behind her. If her finger hadn't throbbed so, she might have lied.

"I'm afraid I'm hooked," she mumbled without turning.

"You've hooked a fish?"

"No, I've hooked my finger," she moaned through clenched teeth.

"If you will stay where you are, I'll be right back to help."

That was an encouraging thought, but having seen the large collection of fishing hooks displayed on the Clinic wall, Kate didn't think this was a job for a handyman.

She was right. Kate hadn't moved. She was too angered and too pained to move. But in what seemed a very short time, she felt the paddleboat being moved back alongside the dock. Swiftly, Paul Dubois cut the line, and with amazing strength hoisted Kate out of the boat and guided her to a lawn chair by the guesthouse porch. Kate was grateful to be seated. For some foolish reason, she was beginning to feel faint.

Paul Dubois studied her face and asked gently. "Outside of the pain, how do you feel?"

"I've felt a lot better," Kate replied weakly, and then noticed he was opening a vaguely familiar looking black bag.

Seeing the surprised look on Kate's face, Paul Dubois explained, "Mrs. Stenson, I think I owe you an apology. The other day I should have introduced myself as Dr. Paul Dubois."

Perhaps it was the pain, perhaps it was the unexpected revelation, but whatever the cause, Kate suddenly felt light headed, slightly nauseous, and slowly drifting away from reality.

When the world became clear once again, Kate's position had changed. She was now stretched out on a couch on the guesthouse screened porch. She noticed a large band-aid on her right index finger, and could see Paul Dubois, that is, Dr. Paul Dubois, on the phone. He put down the receiver and headed her direction.

"Welcome back." A smile lit his dark eyes. Then his manner became professional. "Mrs. Stenson, I've been trying to reach your husband, but I've gotten no answer."

Kate attempted to raise her head, but weakly decided against it. Her voice quavered. "For telephone directory purposes I've kept my husband's name, but I've been widowed for over a year."

"Is there someone else I should call?"

She was tempted to tell him she had a cat he could call. Instead she tried convincing herself. "No, I'll be just fine. I'm sorry to be such a wimp. I get that way whenever I see blood. Especially my own."

Dr. Dubois pulled a chair closer to the couch. Taking Kate's wrist in his large warm hand, he checked her pulse. That was when Kate knew why the caretaker role hadn't fit. It was his hands. They were soft and well-groomed, not toughened by outdoor work.

"Mrs. Stenson, I think you're ready for some good news. I may have the answer to your wayward cat." Kate's eyes brightened. "Is there a reason you call her Twin?"

"Oh, yes. She has a sister, Little Twin, who could be her double except for a ring of white that circles her neck. But that cat left a year ago, shortly after she was spayed."

"I'm glad to hear that." Kate frowned. Dr. Dubois chuckled. "I mean I'm glad there are two cats. I was beginning to think I was seeing double."

It was Kate's turn to smile. In fact she was beginning to feel better all over. "You mean you've seen both cats?"

"I have. At your suggestion, I put a can of tuna fish by the garage yesterday morning, and by noon I kept seeing one cat after another. Now I know why. I would have called you yesterday, but I saw you had company."

"Oh, those were my son Kent's children, Matthew and Courtney. It was Matthew who was so impressed with your fishing skill. Kent and his family live in Lake Crystal. My daughter and her family live downstate." Kate realized she was rattling on telling much more than was necessary.

She was relieved when Dr. Dubois continued, "On the subject of children, it is my daughter and her family who will be using the main house next week. That is one of the reasons I bought this place. It's half way between Ann's home in Minneapolis and my place in Illinois."

Dr. Dubois paused before adding almost inaudibly, "My wife, Sue, died two years ago." Kate caught something more than sadness in his eyes. He changed the subject abruptly, his tone professional again.

"Mrs. Stenson, have you had a tetanus shot? With all your wild cats, it's a good idea."

"I had a booster just last week, as a matter of fact."

"Good. Your pulse and color are back to normal, but I'm going to drive you home just the same. We'll take your fishing gear along. I'll return your paddleboat later."

Kate felt a bit like a recalcitrant child being dismissed after a misdeed. On the trip home she became more than a little uncomfortable with all the opening of doors and solicitous attention. His impeccable manners reminded her of Ben Gessler. Certainly, she thought, with Dr. Dubois, beside manners would not be a problem. Kate flushed at the double-entendre. Just before he left, Dr. Dubois took an envelope out of his pocket and handed it to her.

"I almost forgot. This is the fishhook you were looking for." He opened the flap and Kate peered inside. "As you can see, I've included a few extras to make it easier the next time you lose one."

"Thank you, doctor." Kate tilted her head up and matched his mischievous grin. "I think I've learned my lesson."

After she closed the front door, Kate's first move was to phone the beauty shop. Amber sensed a mood change, and stayed clear of her path. "Vera, could you squeeze me in sometime today? Thanks."

While Kate's feelings were still ripe, she went directly to her notebook.

Day Six

Dear Ben,

Doctors! I don't know whether to hug them or hit them. You wanted me to get in touch with my feelings. Thanks a lot! Now I'm an emotional yo-yo. Today I don't know whether to laugh or cry. And why do I have this uneasy feeling that you doctors are not through with me yet? No more letter writing. Tomorrow I meet you face to face, so watch out!

AMBER KNOWS BEST

Chapter Eight

Both Kate and Amber slept soundly and awoke refreshed and full of energy. Like a Durelco Dance duo, they waltzed through their breakfast routine, and then went their separate ways. No more letters of food logs, Kate decided. Action. That's what she needed. Kate's wish for a walking partner had unexpectedly materialized. Her church friend, Martha Kline, had called yesterday evening worrying about this year's Church School Christmas Program.

"Let's walk on it," Kate suggested. "For some reason, my mind works better when my legs are moving."

Martha lived across the highway that divided the town, so the two agreed to meet at Railroad Street as a starting point. Martha's thoughts were in gear the moment the two met.

"Every year our Christmas programs seem to get more difficult – finding suitable material, finding time to rehearse, and hardest of all, finding someone who will be in charge of the whole mess -- I mean production."

They had only walked half a block, and already Kate was panting. Martha definitely had the age, weight, and leg advantage. Fortunately for Kate, an idea surfaced that slowed them both down. "I may have just been struck with a heaven-sent inspiration."

"Hallelujah," Martha whooped. "Let me hear it."

"This problem seems insurmountable because the church school program is always in competition with the choir concert, Advent family nights, and a trillion other holiday activities. Right?"

Martha's upbeat mood plummeted. "Yeah, sure. Show me how that can be done amicably, and I've got the solution for peace between a Viking and a Packer fan."

Kate picked up their pace and her explanation. A children's Christmas musical had been mixed in with her church school materials last Sunday, and Kate had read it Monday night as a sedative for her frustrating day. To her surprise, it turned out to be a fresh mix of a contemporary story and setting, with flash backs of the nativity scenes, all wrapped around some very singable songs.

"The more I think about it, Martha, we might create a mini-Oberammergau right here in Lake Crystal by combining the adult choir, church school kids – in fact, by getting all the families working together and presenting it as a Christmas gift to the community."

"You know, Kate, it just might work."

* * *

By the time Kate got back home again, she was in such a rush to get in the house and put her feet up, she almost overlooked a small, white bag lodged inside the entryway screen door. She scooped it up and deposited it on the island counter, as she poured herself some iced tea from the refrigerator.

An open bag was an invitation to play. Amber, with his face inside the parcel, quickly pushed this toy off the counter and onto the floor before Kate had replaced the ice cube tray. A box of Snoopy Band-Aids lay next to the bag.

"What's this, Amber? For goodness sakes, who's sending us medical supplies?" On cue, Amber nosed over the bag revealing the writing on one side. Picking up the bag, band-aids, and Amber, Kate curled up on the loveseat rocker, and straightened out the paper to more easily decipher the words scrawled in black pen. Immediately Amber moved onto Kate's lap, purring for attention.

"OK, Amber. I'll read what it says: 10 a.m. Dear Mrs. Stenson, I'm sorry I missed you this morning. I wanted to be sure your finger was healing properly. I also came begging a favor. My daughter, Ann, and her family are arriving tomorrow for a week, and I wonder if my two grandsons, Brian (9) and Bruce (11), might use your paddleboat sometime during their stay. Neighborly yours, PD.

"Tomorrow?" Kate suddenly sat ramrod straight. "The Dubois family is arriving tomorrow? Amber, we'd better hop to it and get our baking done this afternoon or your idea of a thank you gift will be too late."

In record time Kate had made a double batch of frosted chocolate bars for the kids and several dozen old fashion soft molasses cookies – Reed's favorite – for the adults. While the molasses cookies cooled, she bathed and put on the same sweater and blue slacks that garnered compliments when she wore them to the grade school and clinic.

With the cookies and bars packed in separate canisters, and stacked in Kate's light weight nylon carry-all bag, she walked down the south hill toward the guest house. At the bottom of the hill she paused by the creek. The water level was low this time of year, but in the spring it often overflowed its banks. As Kate leaned against the curved wooden railing of the bridge, watching the sun reflect on rivulets below, she remembered an earlier time, before there was a bridge.

A split rail fence erected by the original owners used to divide the properties, but there was far more than a fence separating these two families. Charles and Mary Madden lived at their lake home only three months of the year. They used their property during the summer primarily as a place for Charles to entertain the wealthy friends who served with him on the various boards and foundations he headed.

Kate had heard from the town gossips that Charles Madden still had the first nickel he ever made. Harold Johnson, a native of Lake Crystal, would agree. He was caretaker for Lake Crystal Lodge for twenty years, and let it be known that he never was paid more than $1.10 an hour. For this princely sum, Harold felled trees, cut the ten acres of lawn, put in and took out docks, kept the flower gardens in shape, plus lots of extras that "old man Madden tacked on to his daily job lists."

The Maddens had no children, so the Stenson children ventured on their manicured property only when they had to retrieve an errant ball that rolled beyond the fence.

Some years later, when the Hellman's bought the property, things changed. Kate smiled now as she recalled the first time she met Judy Hellman. It was a warm day in early June, and Kate was adding some fertilizer to the planters on the south deck in preparation for transplanting some marigolds and petunias. She didn't notice her new neighbor approaching the creek.

"Hello!" Judy hollered.

Startled, Kate looked up to see a round-faced, pretty brunette in her early forties standing by the creek's edge. Kate returned her smile and walked down the hill towards the fence.

"I'm Judy Hellman. We bought the Madden place, and I'm curious about these green plants growing in the creek. Are they weeds or what?"

"Hi Judy. I'm glad to meet you. I'm Kate Stenson." Kate leaned over the fence. "I can't quite tell from this distance, but I think it's watercress. I've never had any, but I've heard watercress sandwiches are quite tasty."

"That's right. I remember my mother telling me about that when I was a kid in Indiana."

From their first meeting, Kate and Judy had hit it off. Not only did they share a Hoosier heritage, they both shared a love of their adopted home in the north woods. It wasn't long before the split rail fence was removed from that portion of the Hellman property nearest the two homes. Shortly after that the Hellmans built a four-foot wide plank bridge across the creek and the Hellmans and the Stenson provided steady two-way traffic over that small connecting thoroughfare. In the winter, when the creek was frozen, Kate and her grandkids would start their sled run from the top of the hill on the Stenson property, then head across the bridge to the Hellman's side.

It occurred to Kate as she crossed the bridge today, that the Dubois family might extend the split rail fence to the lake once again, and halt that fun family activity.

She could see Dr. Dubois' truck in the large garage, and paused between the two houses debating which way to go.

"Hello there." Kate jumped, then smiled at her schoolgirl reaction to his friendly greeting. "Come in, come in." The doctor held open the back door of the main house, motioning Kate inside the kitchen.

Kate laid the containers on the kitchen table. "Dr. Dubois, these are ..."

"Please, call me Paul," he interrupted. "I hung up my stethoscope two years ago," Then he smiled and added, "Except for minor surgeries like fishhook extractions." He picked up the canisters and sniffed their freshly baked contents. "Mm! I think I smell chocolate and molasses."

Kate laughed. "You're absolutely right. And please call me Kate. I haven't hung up my spatula yet. But except for visits from the grandchildren, I don't bake as much as I used to. Oh, before I forget, Paul, your grandsons are quite welcome to use the paddleboat whenever they like. You should go for a ride yourself. It's not just a kid sport. Reed and I used to take trips around the island four or five times a summer." Paul was looking at Kate now in a way that made her a bit uncomfortable. "Speaking of family, I should be getting back home. My son made arrangements to have a load of firewood delivered this afternoon."

Paul intercepted her sudden move to the door. "Before you go, Kate, let me see how your finger is healing."

She watched Paul tenderly inspect her finger, and felt an overpowering pity for those patients who no longer received his care. Kate sensed there was a good bit about Paul Dubois that she didn't know, and perhaps didn't want to know.

AMBER KNOWS BEST

Chapter Nine

"Look at me, Amber. I can't tell this story to the back of your head." Amber was Kate's audience as she told about a shepherd boy who cried wolf once too often. Granted, the word "wolf" seemed to elicit some cat reaction, but nothing else did. The phone rang.

You've just been saved by the bell, Puss Puss. " Kate opened the back door, and nudged his furry rump. "Go out on the porch and watch the bird feeder for awhile."

Kate had barely said "hello" before Kerrie was off and whining.

"We've only been in Phoenix for a day, and I'm bored with apartment living already. Help!" Kerrie pleaded.

"I need some excitement or at least some gossip. What's the latest on your new neighbors? Have you met them?"

"One of them."

"Which one?"

Kate twisted the phone cord around her finger as she teased her friend. "The caretaker who isn't."

"Kate, you goose! Make sense."

"Remember the gentleman I saw getting out of the truck the last time you called?"

"Yes," Kerrie prompted. "Go on."

"Well, I finally got to meet him face to face—actually it was more like back to face. It was more than a bit embarrassing to be caught trespassing on their property.

"Oh, that's too complicated to explain, but at least I got his name. It's Paul Dubois. Rather, that's the name he gave me that day."

"That day? Kate," Kerrie complained. "I think you've been out in the sun too long."

Kate continued her monologue, unfazed by Kerrie's interruptions. "A few days later Paul and I met under quite different circumstances, and I got caught again---well, not caught, exactly. I'd say I got hooked."

"HOOKED!" Kerrie gasped.

After Kerrie's last outburst, Kate could no longer continue her story with a straight face. Still, by the end of her explanation, her friend was more than a little impressed with Paul's physician status.

"A doctor. Well, the neighborhood is looking up. OK, Kate, this is good so far, but I need more details. What is the doctor like? I mean, why is he doing yard work, for goodness sake. And since you've seen him up close, I need a more exact physical description. Details, Kate. I need details."

"I'll try, Sherlock, but I've only been on this case for four days, and there are large holes in my research. Maybe the good doctor

does yard work because it is a welcome change from the operating room. I don't know. As far as physical description goes, do you remember the actor who played Mitzi Gaynor's Frenchman in "South Pacific"?

"He looks like Rossano Brazzi?"

"You'd probably think he was better looking. The doctor is bigger, built more like a football player. He has dark brown kind of brooding eyes, and short, curly gray hair. He doesn't smile much, but when he does, he has dimples that match the cleft in his chin." Kate surprised herself with the detail of her description.

By now Kerrie was ecstatic. "Wow! How about the rest of this gorgeous family? His wife? What can you tell me about her?"

Kate purposely ignored the wife question. "I think some of the family is coming next weekend. I may know more then. How is Donna's house search coming along?"

With Kerrie safely off the Dubois family, Kate kept her friend busy detailing family news the rest of the conversation.

After the verbal exercise, Kate needed some quiet. She joined Amber on the screened in porch, and they watched the diving antics of a pair of grebes swimming in the cove. In contrast to yesterday's cold snap, the breeze felt warm again. The bright orange paddleboat bobbed in place. Twin and Little Twin sat side by side on the boardwalk--another reminder of yesterday. Both had reported in for breakfast this morning.

"Amber, my friend, I need some advice. How can I possibly say 'thank you' to someone who probably has everything?" Amber headed for his food dish.

"Food? Say, that's an idea. I could bake something, and take it over when Dr. Dubois' family is here. Amber, you are an absolute genius. Thank you, sweetie." Kate scooped up her pet and headed for the bedroom. "I just may give you a few more crunchies for that good advice."

She sorted through her Courtney-arranged closet for a suitable storytelling outfit, and decided on a bright red sweater and a pair of navy slacks that had been put on the 'give away' pile last week, and for some reason seemed loose enough today. The long, door mirror pictured some differences from the grubby Tug Boat Annie it had reflected the day before. Certainly the haircut and shampoo brought a new springy sheen to Kate's short, white curls. But there was something else.

Another phone call ended her contemplation. It was Shelby reminding Kate to drop off her food log before her appointment. The clinic and grade school were on the same street—easy walking distance from each other. Most places of business in this small town were within easy walking distance, Kate was finding out. Still, she wished she had a walking partner.

Unlike Amber, Courtney's classmates reacted so enthusiastically to "The Three Billy Goats Gruff," that Kate was persuaded to tell three other of Courtney's favorite stories, and had to jog up the hill to be on time for her clinic appointment.

Shelby asked Kate to get on the scales twice, which seemed an unnecessary humiliation. Kate didn't look or ask what she weighed. Her own scales were conveniently gathering dust under her bed, where they had been pushed two years ago.

After the weigh-in, Kate was ushered back to Ben Gessler's office and told it would be only a few minutes. She was looking out the window at the sunlit splashed maple and birch leaves, when Ben came in and stood beside her chair.

"I like what I see," Ben remarked.

I like what I see, too," Kate agreed. "Fall is my favorite season."

"I mean you, Kate. You're looking great." He took a piece of paper out of the folder. "I see Shelby has put a note by your weight which reads, 'Please find out from Kate how she did it.'"

Kate was a little surprised. "Have I lost weight?"

"Five pounds. Looking over your food long, I can see at least part of the reason. The second day your food quantity is reduced. What was the reason for that?"

"My cat, Amber."

Ben raised his eyebrows. "Your cat?"

"I have an unhealthily fat cat. His doctor recommended a cut back on quantity. When I compared my day's rations with Amber's, I cut back, too. I haven't changed what I eat, just how much.

"I did make one exception. I had to cut out Snicker candy bars completely. I discovered I'm a Snicaholic."

"Wise lady. Anything else I should tell Shelby?"

"I started taking walks."

"Whose good idea was that?"

"It's called 'getting your mind on something else.' I used to hate it when my mother said 'Just get your mind on something else' whenever I would complain about something. I have to admit that in this case she was sure right. Whenever I am tempted to double my food intake, I just get up and get going—the faster the better.

He walked toward his desk chair. "How about the journals?"

"Didn't you get my letters?"

Before Ben could respond, Kate explained the reason for her letter format, and the emotional roller coaster that it spawned. She worried aloud where this new vulnerability would lead.

Ben responded honestly. "Kate, I don't know all the answers. I DO know that you are heading in the right direction, and I'm here to help you on your journey back to good health." To reinforce that last statement, Ben set up an appointment in two weeks, and gave Kate some final dieting advice.

"Don't forget to drink seven or eight glasses of water daily, and also don't expect a five pound loss next week. One to two pounds is a better rate."

"Ben, it's not a cosmetic thing with me. If I lose more weight doing what I'm doing, fine. I just want to be able to keep up with my grandchildren without panting."

As she passed Ben on her way out of the office, Ben asked, "How did you hurt your finger?"

Kate smiled and winked, "I'll tell you that story next time—maybe."

AMBER KNOWS BEST

Chapter Ten

Kate valued her own privacy. She would never purposely eavesdrop on others. In this case she couldn't avoid it. The Stenson home had been built with a southern exposure, and the wide expanse of living and dining room windows, which overlooked the south end of the lake, also overlooked the Dubois property.

Kate was sitting at the dining room table having lunch when Paul Dubois' family arrived from Minneapolis. She noticed the black and gray Mercury Villager minivan winding through the trees before parking in the turn around close to the buildings. Paul burst from the main house. That same instant, grandsons Brian and Bruce were released from the van's confines. They circled their grandfather in a bear hug, then raced over the acreage like hound dogs in search of prey.

Kate smiled. She could see that her offer of the paddleboat was a top-notch idea. With their boyish exuberance, those young explorers might well map out all seven miles of lake coastline before their vacation time expired.

After his grandsons disappeared from view, and Paul had helped his daughter and son-in-law carry their luggage into the main house, the adults started a walking tour. From Kate's perspective, Ann's husband appeared tall and muscular like her father, Paul. In contrast, Ann was petite and very blond--probably a young version of her mother.

At one point in their ambling, Paul gestured in the direction of the Stenson house. Kate moved slightly away from the windows. "Darn that Kerrie," Kate thought. "She has started me on a very bad habit. At least I wasn't using binoculars."

She watched Paul point to the guesthouse and smile like a proud parent. He had acquired not one but two unique houses. When Judy and Dave Hellman owned the property, the guesthouse was used only occasionally. It had been built in 1932 by Charles Madding, the original owner, at his wife Mary's request. Mary enjoyed having company, but preferred not to cook for them. It was Madding's policy to stock the cabin's kitchen with groceries for their guest's convenience, but also take them out to eat often at the various restaurants in this resort town. In some respects the guest cabin was a small replica of the main house. Both were built from logs cut on the property. The fieldstones used in the foundations and fireplaces had also been mined locally.

The guests invited to the Madding's many lawn parties could enjoy boating, fishing, and a variety of land games – volley ball, shuffle board, horseshoes. They even had a meticulously groomed bowling green next to the outdoor bar. All the areas were flooded with light when the parties continued into the night. Kate and Reed were occasionally invited to these soirees, but the Stensons did not travel in the same social circles as the Maddings, nor did they care to.

The Maddings had sold the property, with all the lawn toys, to the Hellmans, and obviously Paul Dubois had been offered the same deal. Kate could see the grandsons had found the shuffleboard equipment, and were full of whoops and hollers as the competition intensified.

Kate stood puzzling. Less than two weeks ago she had been delighted that his property was devoid of human occupants. Today she felt curiously content over just the opposite situation. Maybe it was the vagaries of the season. Kate had always loved fall in Lake Crystal. Even with her tortoise-like metabolism, she experienced an urgency to accomplish something. The shorter days and colder temperatures were a foretaste of the coming winter. So each autumn day of warmth and leaf color was a bonus to be experienced with a miser's care.

She had better things to do than watch the Dubois family activities. For the next several days, Kate and Martha formulated their plans for the church Christmas musical. Martha, who was a choir member, would tactfully present the idea to that august group. Once she had extracted their approval, Kate would initiate tryouts for the major speaking roles.

Costuming this production would be a harder hurdle to vault. There were some "make-do" items on hand, but since every church school student – ages three to thirteen – would be part of the cast, the job needed a professional hand.

"I know someone we could ask," Martha chirped. "Greta Paulson. All three of her kids were ice skaters, and one time she made forty snowflake costumes for the kindergarten chorus line."

"Bingo!" Kate echoed. "I'll catch her on the way out of church this Sunday."

Kate and Martha found other reasons to converse on these morning treks. Martha had two teenagers: Crystal, who was a fashion freak and thought school was divine, and Bruce who would rather eat snakes than open a book. Having already been through that war with her own kids, Kate could be a compassionate sounding board for Martha's frustration.

Between her daily walks with Martha, letter writing to Kerrie, Kate's sister Kathryn, her own daughter Jill, and the usual weekly get-togethers with her son's family, Kate's days were increasingly busy.

Sunday, after the kids left, Kate plopped on the sofa to peruse the newspaper. She read the serious issues of the day followed by Erma and Abby, then sensed something was wrong. It was just a subliminal feeling for a while; then the truth surfaced. No Amber. The rustle of the newspaper should have brought him running. Next to eating, hop scotching on the paper strewn on the floor was his favorite pastime.

Now there was paper temptingly covering the sofa and floor, but no sign of Amber to take the bait. Why? That's what Kate aimed to find out. She searched his haunts and hideouts and finally found him under the guest room bed, sulking. She knew it was a sulk because he turned his head away from her when she crawled under the narrow passage to pull him out.

Kate and Amber had been bosom buddies too long for Kate not to know why he was hurt. Up to two weeks ago, Amber had fulfilled Kate's every need. He was her confidante and closest friend. But slowly that was beginning to change. Kate was turning to others while Amber was left alone.

This wasn't the first time Amber had felt the cold fingers of neglect. When Reed befriended the outside kittens, much of his time was spent on their care and supervision. Amber spent hours soulfully watching from every window of the house as Reed attended to the wild ones. That was the one time in Amber's life that he was "off his feed." Kate shared this observation with Reed, who immediately made a conscious effort to make amends. But it was too late. After that, Amber was Kate's cat.

By his actions now, Kate knew that Amber felt he was losing even her. Kate dragged her cat from his dark under-bed hermitage. She held him close and was shocked by his obvious weight loss. She returned to the living room couch nuzzling, petting, and offering soft words of consolation to her pet.

"Amber, my dear friend. I owe you my deepest apology." When Amber tried to turn away, Kate held his head still and looked deep into his golden tan eyes.

"You know I absolutely could not have survived this year without your love and tender care. Day and night you were always here for me." She scratched his nose with her thumb. "Your warm, soft, furry body blotted my tears many a long night after Reed died." Kate pushed her wet face into Amber's fur now, and hugged him close – swaying back and forth until she felt his body relax and his purring begin. After a while she draped Amber's body over her chest.

"Thank you, my dear Amber," Kate murmured as they both slipped into the comforting sleep of the forgiven.

Chapter Eleven

The phone's sharp jangle pierced the living room silence, sending Amber under the couch, and Kate scrambling groggily to her feet to answer its call. Still in a sleepy fog, Kate only half-listened to the soft female voice until she identified herself as Ann Richardson, Paul Dubois' daughter.

"I hope I haven't disturbed you, Mrs. Stenson."

"Not at all, Kate fibbed. My grandchildren left not too long ago, and I'm just catching up on some reading."

"Would you object to some company? All my guys are busy. Brian and Bruce are off paddling around the lake somewhere in your dandy boat, and Don and Dad are out on the dock trying their luck at fishing."

Kate moved toward the window and could see that was indeed the case. "Please come ahead. I'd enjoy meeting you, Ann."

The same time she graciously issued this invitation, Kate frantically looked around to see what kind of crash clean up job she'd have before the guest arrived. Except for the Sunday paper scattered about, the house was actually quite presentable. Maybe Courtney was right. This past week Kate had been trying to live up to the advice her young granddaughter, the Grand Duchess of Housekeeping, espoused. "Gramma, Mother says an orderly house reflects an orderly mind."

Kate had a fresh pot of coffee brewing by the time she saw Ann Richardson heading across the bowling green swinging a colorful plaid canvas bag in one hand. With a speed she hadn't known she possessed, Kate was downstairs and outside, directing Ann to come in the family room entrance. The garage still did not pass Courtney's high standards, and certainly would not make a good first impression. Kate held open the door, and Ann sailed through like a fresh breeze. As she passed, Kate thought of Reed and his eye for feminine pulchritude. "A natural beauty." That's how Reed would have described her. "A head-turner everywhere she goes."

Ann's sun-bleached blond hair was pulled back in a ponytail, and tied with a bright pink chiffon scarf. The same pink accented the collar, cuffs and belt of her otherwise all white blouse and slacks outfit. The total effect would have sent Crystal, Martha's fashion freak daughter, into orbit.

As Kate led the way through the family room and upstairs, Ann found something to admire at every level. First the red, white, and pink blooms of the geraniums and begonias lining the downstairs bay windowsill caught her eyes. Then she paused at the landing to touch the country-blue shelf supporting the tall walnut clock.

"I love the warmth of walnut. You must enjoy antiques as much as I do."

Kate nodded. "That was a very special gift from my father who fixed clocks and watches as a hobby. It's an 1837 Chauncey Jerome." As if on cue, the clock struck three times.

"What a mellow sound."

"Reed and I thought so too, when we put it in our bedroom. After one night of counting off the hours, we moved it here." They both chuckled.

All chatter stopped when Ann reached the main room.

"What a magnificent view!" She moved closer to the windows. "Oh, look. I think I can see the boys way down by the mouth of the river." She turned to Kate. "If this were my house, I'd never leave this spot."

Kate smiled. "Some days I have that problem, especially this time of year."

Ann pointed toward the Dubois dock and squealed. "Look, Don's caught a fish. What kind is it?"

"A smallmouth bass I'd imagine. They like to hide in the lily pads and weeds this time of year." Kate motioned to the dining room table. "Sit here, Ann, where you can watch all the action, and I'll pour us some coffee."

Only then did Ann remember her excuse for coming, and took the canisters from her bag. "Mrs. Stenson, your delicious bars and cookies were life savers. When we got here Thursday there was so much to talk about and see, we didn't want to stop for supper. So I just made a fresh pot of coffee, got some milk for the boys, and we feasted on your homemade bars and goodies till they were almost gone."

Dock activity captured Ann's attention again. "Now Dad's got a fish. Oh just look at him smile." Suddenly Ann turned away, and put her hands over her mouth, choking back tears. Kate was unprepared for this sudden switch from joy to sorrow.

"I'm sorry." Ann fought for control. "It's just that it has been two years since I've seen Dad truly happy. I was beginning to despair that he ever would be again."

The silence stood heavy between them, like a wall. Hoping to break the barrier and ease her pain, Kate gave Ann soft encouragement. "Ann, your father mentioned that he retired from his medical practice two years ago."

Ann nodded. "Everyone tried to talk him out of it, but his guilt was just too great."

"Guilt?"

This word unleashed the sad narrative of Ann's mother, Sue, and her battle with lung cancer.

"From the very beginning of their lives together, Dad tried to persuade Mom to stop smoking. But, whenever she did, she would gain weight, or there would be some other excuse she had for continuing." Ann looked up at Kate, her light green eyes glazed with tears. "Do you smoke, Mrs. Stenson?"

Kate shook her head.

"Me neither. I begged Mom to stop, but she said she couldn't-- even when she knew she had cancer." Ann's voice was bitter.

There were still unanswered questions, so Kate quietly probed. "Ann, you mentioned guilt."

"Yes. Mom didn't want to die in the hospital. So, when all the treatments had been tried and failed, Dad got round the clock home nursing care for Mom, and reduced his patient load to be home with her. Mom made Dad promise he'd be with her when the end came. That is where the guilt comes in.

"Dad's specialty was obstetrics. Before Mom got real sick, he had a patient, Helen Maxwell, who had miscarried four times. Finally, with Dad's help, she had carried full term. But in the last week of her pregnancy, complications developed, and Helen's husband, Jeff, begged Dad to come to the hospital. While Dad was saving the life of a mother and her long awaited baby, his own wife of thirty five years died." Emotions threatened to overpower Ann once again. "He wasn't with Mom, and he has never forgiven himself. "I'm certain Mom didn't know he wasn't there, but Dad had broken their promise."

Kate put her hand on Ann's arm, too moved to speak herself. It would have been an awkward moment had not Amber come to the rescue. Evidently, as Ann told her story, Amber had moved out from under the couch to listen. This was a pretty woman in obvious distress who needed comforting, so he took action. When Amber jumped in Ann's lap, she was virtually surprised out of her sorrow.

"Oh, you gorgeous creature," she gushed. "Where did you come from?" That compliment was all Amber needed to settle in Ann's lap for more. The cat purred, Ann scratched his forehead, and Kate feigned dismay. "I don't know what has come over Amber. He usually does not appear when guests arrive."

"Amber is it?" Ann stroked his back. "You know, Amber, you look a good bit like Casanova, the cat Dad had before Mom got so sick."

Before the subject changed completely, there was still a missing link in the Paul Dubois puzzle, so Kate inquired further. "Ann, your father mentioned that his home was in Illinois, and you folks live in Minneapolis. What brought Paul to northern Wisconsin?

Ann paused before answering. "Now that I look back on it, I'd call it Providence. Dad and his close friend, Jerry Walker, had interned together at St. Lukes in Duluth. Jerry stayed in the area while Dad went back to Illinois and started a practice in Hinsdale. But Jerry and Dad always kept in touch, went on fishing tips together once a year. Judy and Doug Hellman and Jerry and his wife, Nancy, were good friends. So when the Hellman's mentioned to Jerry that they were buying a condominium in the Virgin Islands and wanted to sell their place in Lake Crystal, with everything in it, he thought of Dad. He and Dad had gone on a Canadian fishing trip and Jerry could tell Dad needed a big change in his life." Ann pointed to the Dubois property. "That is it." Turning back to Kate, Ann added. "And now he even has a friend next door to keep him company." Kate flushed, Ann giggled and then turned serious again. "Mrs. Stenson, our time with Dad has been too short. He wanted the kids to see his place, but we can't keep them out of school much longer. Hopefully, we'll all be back for Christmas. Dad's promised to check out the airport south of town to see if they have facilities for Don's private plane." She gave Amber a hug. "I've far overstayed my welcome."

Ann rose to leave, then stopped abruptly and came back to where Kate stood. "Mrs. Stenson, thank you for being such a wonderful listener. I'm not at all sure Dad would have wanted me to tell you about Mom. You are the first person I've really been able to talk to about my feelings. I certainly don't want Brian and Bruce to hear me talk this way." Impulsively she reached out and hugged Kate. "I'm not usually a hugger either." Before Kate could respond, Ann was headed toward the stairs. "You don't need to see me out. Thanks again for the coffee, and for being a friend for Dad."

Kate picked up Amber and watched from the window as Ann joined the men on the dock. Ann spoke briefly to Paul and Don, and then they all turned toward the Stenson house and waved. Kate watched as the trio headed, arm in arm, toward the main house.

"Amber, there goes a family with a problem. You and I know that forgiving someone else is very hard – but forgiving yourself? How can you do that?"

AMBER KNOWS BEST

Chapter Twelve

The call to be Paul's friend came sooner than Kate expected. The morning after Ann and family left, Paul was on the phone asking Kate out to lunch at the Skyport Restaurant south of town.

Part of Kate wanted to state firmly and flatly, "No thank you. I've got a dozen squirrelly grade school kids coming to the church after school today to tryout for the Christmas musical. I plan to do nothing between now and then but laze around the house and drink spinach juice to build up my energy."

The other part chastised, "Shame on you! You know how let down you feel when Jill and her family head south after a visit. How could you be such a Hard-Hearted Hannah?" Her Dr. Jekyll side won over, and she agreed to go.

This wasn't a date, she told herself, yet she spent more time than usual deciding what to wear. At her appointment with Ben, Monday, the scales had registered another two-pound loss. This allowed more clothes options.

With her weight loss had come a little more interest in how she looked. Kate also conceded that Courtney had better fashion sense than she, so she listened when her granddaughter commented on Sunday, "Gramma, that's a pretty color sweat on you. And you know something else? I think your butt's getting smaller."

"Hips, Courtney," Kate had corrected. "And thank you."

Only her son Kent objected to her change of eating style. It was his habit to raid the cookie jar and refrigerator whenever he came to do Kate's handyman chores. Now on these visits he'd complain, "There's never anything good to eat around here anymore." He was right. Kate wasn't baking like she used to, because she still had little self-control as far as sweets were concerned. If they were in the house, she'd devour them.

The sweater Courtney liked was a teal cardigan, so Kate chose that to wear today over a white shirt and a pair of almost new jeans. She had purchased the jeans just before Reed died, and had quickly eaten her way out of them this past year.

Ready ahead of time, Kate was just going out the door to chat with the outside cats when the phone rang. It was Kerrie. She demanded, "So, what's new in your life." Knowing she expected the ritual answer "Nothing – what's new with you," Kate's newly emerged Mr. Hyde reared its voice again.

With a newfound boldness, she quickly clipped, "What's new? Let's see. I've taken your advice: cleaned my house, gotten back in shape, and am just heading to lunch with the handsome doctor next door."

"Whaaaat?" screeched Kerrie. "What about his wife?"

"Sorry." Kate's voice was evilly sweet. "I can't talk anymore now, but I promise to write you all about it – when I have time." She hung up the phone hearing Kerrie's howls, then got outside quickly before Kerrie could call her back. She worried just a bit about this dark side of her character beginning to surface. Ann Richardson had talked about the anger she felt over her mother's untimely death. Kate could understand that feeling. She still felt angry with Reed for leaving her alone, even though he had done nothing to precipitate the series of strokes that eventually caused his death.

Fortunately, the outside cats quickly diverted her attention. Boots, always Reed's favorite, came first, rubbing his long-haired calico body against her legs. As Kate sat down in Reed's chair, assertive Blackie appeared demanding attention by jumping up on her lap, then purring loudly as he snuggled close. The Twins marched single file out of the woods to the north and sat close enough for petting. Paul evidently pulled his pickup by the garage, and Kate didn't notice him until he walked around the house. His presence startled all the cats except Blackie, who remained in Kate's lap and responded graciously to Paul's gentle petting and salutation. "Hello there, Blackie."

"How did you know his name?"

Paul effortlessly squatted down beside the chair and continued stroking the handsome black and white animal. "I didn't. I just knew that is what I'd have named him if he were my cat. I bet Blackie gets what he wants."

Kate laughed. "You are quite right. In fact he has me in his clutches right now, and the trick will be getting out of them."

As Kate stood, Paul carefully disengaged Blackie's claws, a job easier because the cat had to give some attention to this strange, but friendly, handler. The other cats stayed at a distance, but seemed unafraid. Kate noted their trust and thought them a good judge of character.

Paul led the way, and with an exaggerated waist bow, opened the passenger door of a 1976 Ford pickup. This vehicle had obviously seen heavy-duty service, which is what made Paul's straight-faced invitation so humorous. "Your carriage awaits, Madame."

Taking his cue, Kate responded with a curtsy. "Dr. Dubois, you are so kind. But Madame has been cursed with short legs, so I fear that first step is beyond my reach."

"Never fear, Madame, just put your arms on my shoulders and I'll transport you into the limousine." Kate did as she was directed. With apparent ease she was delivered to her seat. Enroute however, she contracted a serious case of the giggles, and the infection spread to Paul. As a consequence, they did little more than laugh their way to the restaurant. Paul did mange to explain the reason for the pickup.

"I was visiting my friend, Jerry Walker, in Duluth, when the final deal for the lake property came through. Jerry's son was going off to college, and graciously lent me this relic so I could get a few things done before the kids came."

"Actually, you're right in style," Kate assured him. "The junker pickup is the vehicle of choice for many of the town residents." As she spoke, a pickup of an even earlier vintage passed them loaded with an assortment of rubbish. "That's the dump road just ahead. And up the hill on your right is the restaurant."

Paul shifted into third as they neared the crest of the hill, and turned into the almost empty parking lot. He was quick to reach Kate's door and lift her down. He was slow, however, to take his hands from her waist, and Kate knew the reason was not her irresistible charm. For the first time, Paul was viewing Lake Crystal, as the early settlers traveling north must have seen it. From this high spot the river flowing through the valley below looked like a ribbon, and Lockhart's Island, a small green mound rising from a sea of blue.

"I gather you've never approached our town from this direction."

Kate's word broke Paul's trance. "You are right. I might have moved to Lake Crystal sooner if I had. Paul turned to Kate, "Is that the island we can see from our property?"

Kate nodded. "There is quite a story connected with that spot." It was generally breezy on this hill, and now there was more than a chilly edge to the early October air. Kate shivered and pulled the sides of her sweater together as they walked toward the building. Paul put his arm around Kate's shoulders and the warmth of his body felt good to her.

Inside, Kate led Paul past the bar and back to a small pine-paneled room with a large window overlooking the lake. There was a fire in the corner wood stove. The owner's wife, Marie, came quickly with the menus. Kate guessed she would be cook today as well. After Labor Day, midweek lunch business was mighty slim in all but the downtown restaurant. That one caught all the coffee drinkers, local business people, and tourists shopping for the day.

As Paul studied the menu, Kate studied Paul. Today his tanned complexion and almost white hair was enhanced by an amber crew-neck sweater over a white turtleneck. He was handsome, without question, yet there was no hint of vanity in his manner. Kate wondered what prompted his choice of a medical career. He appeared to be as much at home in Lake Crystal as he might be in affluent Hinsdale, yet they were culturally and socially miles apart. Paul looked up and Kate realized he had caught her staring.

He smiled and winked. "What's the matter Kate? Did I shave off a sideburn? It was dark in the bathroom when I got up to see the kids off this morning."

Kate blushed and cleared her throat, "I was admiring your sweater. Reed had one the same color. It was his favorite."

"Well then, that's three things I admire about your husband – his taste in clothes, pets, and ..." Marie returned for their order before Paul could finish.

Chapter Thirteen

After Paul and Marie exchanged lunch orders and airport information, Paul flashed a smile as bright as the freshly lit fire in the corner wood stove. "Looks like I'll get the kids here for the holidays."

Now it was Paul's turn to study Kate's face. His dark brown eyes penetrated hers. "Kate, do you believe in Providence?"

"What do you mean by Providence?"

"That some things are just meant to be." Paul looked out over the river valley. "Coming to Lake Crystal for instance. Why did you and Reed move here, Kate?"

"What if I told you I am a native of these parts?"

"I'd say you are a bit short on the truth."

In mock indignation, Kate raised her eyebrows. "Really sir, on what grounds do you doubt my veracity?"

"Your manner of speaking. I'd say your folks come from further south – Iowa, Illinois, or Indiana. What are you Kate, a Hawkeye, Hoosier or Sucker?"

Kate smiled. "I'd say, by the bent of this conversation I'm probably a 'sucker.' Actually, you're very perceptive. Reed and I both came from Indiana. It was a college romance."

"So it was Providence then that you moved to Lake Crystal?"

"If you mean by Providence, God's loving care and help in our lives – yes, it was Providence."

Immediately, Paul's playful mood changed. His eyes narrowed and anger etched his words. "Loving care, you say. Then how do you explain the ugly stuff?"

This was a side of Paul Dubois she had never seen. It frightened her, and yet she could understand his anger. She had asked that question many times. "Don't tell me this is God's will," she had lashed back at a well-meaning friend after her saintly father lost his battle with liver cancer years ago.

The tears that came now were for Paul, not herself. He would have to find his own answer to that question, and the path might not be easy.

Paul's large hands covered hers, "Forgive me Kate, I'm a heartless fool."

Kate used her napkin for a hanky. "Ben would be so proud of me."

"Ben?" Now it was Paul's turn to be confused.

"Dr. Ben Gessler. He thinks pent up emotions are a Pandora's box. He was proud as punch last month when he discovered that I have some – emotions, that is."

Paul's continued silence worried Kate. She also knew this wasn't the time for preaching or platitudes. "Paul, you asked why we moved to Lake Crystal – in one way our coming was similar to yours. You mentioned your good friends, the Walkers, played a part in your move." Paul smiled.

"Friends played a part in our move, too. We came here first on vacation. Our next-door neighbors and best friends in Middleton, the Schmidt's, were great campers. They came often to Lake Crystal to camp at Hanley Woods Park here in town. Have you been through the park?"

Paul shook his head in affirmation. "As a matter of fact I have. I noticed the park sign when I took the grandkids to the Dairy Queen last week. So we drove down to the lake and drank our shakes on a bench by the water. Beautiful spot. I've never seen so many pine trees that size. Why is it called Hanley Woods?"

"The Hanley family moved to Lake Crystal in 1887 from Ohio on a federal land grant the government used back then to reward Civil War Veterans. At the time, this was all wild country, inhabited mostly by Indians. There is a valley west of town still known by the old timers as Chippewa City."

Paul leaned forward expectantly. "So? Go on with your story, Kate.

Did you and Reed pitch a teepee in the park on your first visit?"

"Oh no," Kate giggled. "We're not campers. But – I guess we did pitch a teepee in a way."

Paul raised his eyebrows and Kate rattled on, caught up with her own memories. "We stayed in a motel close to the park, and spent much of the week walking around the area. On one of those walks on a lake road south of the park, we noticed a for sale sign printed on a shoe box and tacked to the front door of a small, hand-hewn log cabin."

"A shoe box?" Paul asked.

"Yeah! Not exactly Century 21. There was a name and a Duluth telephone number scribbled on the sign. On a whim, we decided to check out the cost of real estate in this pretty lake village, so we knocked on the door. We were relieved to find no one was at home and could snoop around the property pretending to be prospective buyers."

Suddenly, Kate stopped and squirmed in her chair. Paul hadn't taken his eyes off of her face, and she wasn't comfortable with such attention. She wished she hadn't worn a sweater. The woodstove, or something else, was making her quite warm.

"And? ... Paul coaxed. "What happened next?"

"The cabin had been built at the top of a hill close to the road. Below it was the lake. We picked our way down over some crude stone steps to the shore. At that point we could see the island."

"Lockhart's Island?" Paul interjected. "Didn't you say there was an interesting story connected with that place?"

"Mrs. Lockhart's husband was nine years old when his parents bought the island back in 1913. It was called both St. John's Island and the Haunted Island then."

"The Haunted Island?" Paul threw back his head and laughed. "That's wonderful. How did it get that name?"

"Well, according to Betty Lockhart, the island's reputation for being haunted dates back to 1832 when a band of Chippewa Indians, villaging on the island, fled to the mainland when it was rumored that the spirit of a murdered tribesman had returned to haunt the island village. Yep, the island has quite a colorful history. The island was even once a popular location for early French and Indian fur traders. It was an ideal place to hide from surprise attacks; and the wild game on the island made it a favorite camping area for the voyageurs."

"Voyageurs! What do you know?" Paul looked out the window where the island was barely visible. "Wait till I tell the kids." Paul turned back to focus on Kate. "I'm sorry. I keep interrupting your story. What happened after your first visit?"

"Actually, it wasn't so much what happened, but what was said. That afternoon, after we walked over every inch of that spring fed hillside, Reed confessed, "You know, Kate, ever since I was a kid I wanted to live on a lake in the north woods of Wisconsin." Kate smiled at Paul, "Obviously, Reed got his wish."

As if on cue, Marie bustled in with fresh coffee and Kate's salad. Maybe it's the coffee, Kate thought, that has me so wound up. She took a sip of ice water and decided to steer the conversation back to Paul.

"The Schmidt's bought a cabin on Cedar Lake just south of here and continue occasional visits to Lake Crystal. Naturally Kerrie was interested in who bought the Hellman's place. First I referred to you as the caretaker. When I added the doctor title to your name, my credibility with Kerrie dropped considerably. I admit you don't look like a caretaker, but frankly, Paul, you don't look like a doctor either." Kate played her game for all it was worth. "If I were casting director at United Artist and had only photographs to guide me, you wouldn't get called to play Dr. Killdare. However, if I were looking for a retired professional linebacker, or a swashbuckling Indiana Jones type, I'd cast you in a minute. Please! Tell me you were these things in another life, and my instincts are right."

Paul's deep laugh echoed off the pine paneling. "OK, Kate. You are right on one score. I was a football player. A football scholarship was my ticket to Med School at the University of Illinois. Before that I was a small town farm boy, more in love with animals than girls. First thought I'd be a vet, but Mom's death changed all that." For a minute Kate thought she saw anger coming back, but he continued with a smile. "Sorry, I've never been an actor, unless you count my role as George in our high school production of 'Our Town'."

Before Kate could ask more questions, Marie bustled in with their food, and small talk rounded out the rest of the meal.

Kate got the "sillys" again on the ride home. "I just love this truck. It reminds me of the 1937 Ford coupe Reed courted me in on campus. That jalopy was called The Run-About, and it lived up to its name. More than once Reed ran out of gas, and he and his Business School buddies had to push it back to the frat house. Reed told me proudly it was the first 'All Weather' vehicle. I understood what he meant when it rained on our first date, and I got royally drenched. "See," he said. "We've got weather inside and out."

"So, you love this truck?" Kate nodded. "I sure wish I'd known that before. I'm afraid I've got bad news for you, Kate. This tin goddess's courtship days are numbered." As if to emphasize his words, Paul pulled up to Kate's garage and turned off the motor. "I'm taking her back to the Walkers this evening before I catch my early morning flight to Hinsdale."

Paul jumped out of the truck, missing the expression on Kate's face. A quick stab of disappointment had changed her mood, and Kate realized it wasn't because of the truck's imminent departure.

But the down-side didn't last long. Paul swung open the door and Kate put her right arm around Paul's neck to steady herself for the long step down. When her feet touched the ground, and before she could remove her arm, Paul put his right arm around her waist and grinned. "May I have this dance?"

Before Kate could respond, he walked her tango fashion to the front door. It was all so unexpected that Kate returned to giggling all over again. "See?" he said, "I can swashbuckle when the occasion warrants."

Kate felt slightly giddy. His closeness opened dormant emotions that she wanted to squelch. "Thank you, kind sir, for a most pleasant interlude." She attempted to move away, but Paul's grip tightened.

For a moment he said nothing; then he spoke quietly.

"Although I never met Reed, by what you have told me about your life together, I know I would have liked him. He was one lucky guy to have you as his wife."

Paul put his hand under her chin and tilted her face up. "Thanks Kate, for bringing laughter back in my life." Bending down, Paul's lips softly brushed her forehead and lips, then he walked around the house, got into his truck and out of sight before Kate could speak.

Chapter Fourteen

Kate leaned against the front door, staring at Reed's lawn chair. The phone rang and she decided not to answer it. Instead, she headed toward the church. There was still an hour before the children were scheduled to arrive for the Christmas musical tryouts. Normally she would have called Martha and they would have walked to the church together. But she hadn't mentioned Paul Dubois to Martha, or anyone else for that matter, and she needed time to sort through her feelings.

Since most of the summer cabins were closed for the season, Kate took a narrow footpath that skirted the back of some of the lake properties. By this secluded route, she would be hidden from the townsfolk, yet have the solace of the water close by. Even so, there were voices from her past hounding her every step through the park and into the village.

"Be a good girl, Kate." How many times had she heard those words as she headed into puberty. She'd never really questioned what her mother meant by being "good." There were few opportunities to be "bad." Back in the forties when she was a teen, most of Kate's dates took place in very public places. The school dances and private parties were heavily chaperoned. No one had cars, so you walked or took city buses to the movies, which were the major source of entertainment.

When it came to knowledge of the opposite sex, Kate was more naïve than most of her girl friends. She and her sister had no brothers. The closest Kate ever came to seeing a nude male was one Saturday during the summer of her junior year of high school. She had won an art scholarship to the John Heron Art Institute, and this particular day they were to sketch a male model. When the model disrobed, wearing nothing but a jock strap, Kate became so distraught she knocked her easel over, and all her drawing supplies clattered to the floor. The instructor thought she had fainted, and allowed her some time out in the hallway to collect herself. Kate never told her mother about that incident, and hid the revealing picture she had sketched.

Now, almost forty-five years later, Kate was still influenced by the early training she had received from this lady. She could hear Mother Spencer's voice as she walked. "You have been widowed barely a year Kate, and this is not a respectable length of time to be seeing another gentleman. What would your children think? What would your dear grandchildren think? You'd best nip this in the bud before you find yourself doing something even more foolish." As Kate neared the church she said aloud, "Yes Mother, I'll try to be a good girl."

Kate was so deep in her own thoughts she didn't notice Martha standing by the church entrance, wildly waving in her direction.

"Am I ever glad to see you," Martha babbled, "When I couldn't

reach you by phone earlier, I thought you were at the church already, so I hot-footed it here. For some reason most of the kids came early, too. Pastor Southwick is downstairs trying to keep them from wrecking the place."

Martha lowered her voice to a whisper as they headed toward the church basement. "He's not the best at handling kids this age." Kate nodded in agreement. She figured their new young pastor was still a bit too polite and serious in his relationship with young people. Kate and Martha both agreed that kids ages eight to twelve like to know who's boss and be disciplined with a liberal dose of humor.

Through the windowed double doors Kate could see Peter Robbins had a chalkboard eraser behind his back, and was going in for the kill. Jack Smith was his target. Kate knew all about Pete's tricks from church school. Grabbing a whistle off the piano, she blew it three times and got the tryouts in full swing before Jack knew what had hit him.

"Mrs. Kline will pass out scripts, and you can read for any part you would like. Mr. Conley will play the grandfather. All the other characters are kids your age."

A gangly young girl with straight brown hair timidly raised her hand. "Mrs. Stenson, I don't read very well."

"That's not a problem, Amy. In our tryouts today we'll be going over and over the same lines. You just jump in whenever you feel comfortable reading a part."

Peter, the freckle faced third grader with the powerful pitching arm, volunteered, "I don't like saying stuff in front of people."

"I'm glad you let me know that, Peter," Kate said with honest concern.

"Look at the top of your script." Several other reluctant readers followed Kate's directions. "Listed there are the characters we need for the nativity scenes. All of these people are important to the story, but they will not have to learn lines."

"I don't like wearing those funny long dresses guys wore back then," Peter grumbled. Martha caught Kate's desperate glance and commented, "Peter, don't I remember that you helped Mrs. Karlen with the grade school musical last spring – working with the spot lights?"

Peter's belligerent attitude began to soften. "Yeah! I'm good at stuff like that."

Kate smiled her appreciation to Martha and picked up on her cue. "I certainly could use that kind of help with our Christmas musical. I need an assistant director."

"Good, Peter! Mrs. Kline has some pencils and three by five cards. Would you please see that everybody puts their name on the top? The names of the characters are listed. Everyone should put a check beside the five speaking and non-speaking parts they would like to play."

Kate knew from past experience that with that arrangement, everyone got a part they wanted – maybe not their first choice, but one that they could handle.

With Peter in a management role, the rest of the tryouts moved smoothly. Martha commented as much when she and Kate walked home.

"You were impressive this afternoon, Kate. I've never seen you so fired up. What did you have for lunch today?"

Kate laughed and privately wished she could tell Martha the whole story. "I did have spinach salad. Maybe that made the difference."

"If I didn't know better, I'd say you're on some kind of high. You've got the pizzazz my daughter, Crystal, gets after she's been on a date with Mr. Perfect."

Kate was glad her turn off was just ahead. Martha's psychic powers were getting too close for comfort. That "high" Martha mentioned was still charging Kate's system as she jogged the complete length of the lake road and arrived at her front door, panting. Amber meowed his "hello" and the phone rang. Lifting her pet to her shoulders, Kate carried the purring fur piece with her, and struggled to settle Amber in her lap as she picked up the receiver.

"Hello," she sighed, easing into the cushioned comfort of the telephone stool.

"Wonderful, you're home."

"Who is this?" The voice was familiar, but since Reed's death Kate never spoke to male callers without positive identification.

"Forgive me, Kate, my mother taught me better manners. This is Paul Dubois." Then he laughed. "Remember me? The fellow with the truck you liked?"

Now it was Kate's turn to chuckle. "Ah, yes. How quickly we forget! I thought you'd be on your way to Duluth by now."

"I'm due at the Walkers at six, but I've got a favor to ask of you. I thought of it after I left your place. When I came back you were gone."

"I had a church meeting and decided to walk off a few of my lunch calories. How can I help you, Paul?" She hoped her voice sounded business-like; her palpitating heart certainly wasn't cooperating.

"Would you keep an eye on my place for me? In Hinsdale, vacant homes are a problem. I'm not sure about Lake Crystal."

"The crime rate is generally low here, but I'll be happy to take note of any strange vehicles I see in your driveway and alert our town constable. Do you know how long you'll be gone?"

"I'll let you know when I know." Paul paused and lowered his voice. "That's not the real reason I called, Kate."

"Oh?" Amber was squirming in Kate's lap. "Excuse me Paul. I've got a hair hunk of a guy in my lap who wants to get down."

"Oh? I'm sorry. I didn't know you had company."

"Really, Mr. Dubois," she intoned mock horror. "The hair hunk I'm referring to is my CAT, Amber. What kind of establishment do you think I'm running here?"

Paul laughed until Kate wasn't sure he would stop. "That's it, Kate. That's the real reason I called. I guess I should say, YOU'RE the real reason I called."

Kate quickly changed the subject, "That's good I guess, but you'd better be on your way if you plan to get to the Walkers by six."

"You're right Kate. Thanks."

From her perch on the phone stool, Kate could see Paul run to the truck. She watched as the truck headed up the hill and out of sight; then she picked up Amber once again. "You know, my friend, I'm not at all sure I'm ready for another man in my life."

Kerrie's telephone call an hour later only reinforced that feeling. "What are you up to?" Kerrie questioned sharply without so much as a salutary "Hello."

"Listen, Kate, when I suggested you needed to put some order back into your life, I didn't mean you should start dating a married man, for goodness sake!"

"It wasn't a date, " Kate countered, in a tone slightly louder and a bit testier than her friend's. "And Paul Dubois is not married. He's a widower."

"How long has he been widowed?" Kerrie demanded.

"Two years. But what difference does that make?"

"It makes a lot of difference. At this point in time both of you are very vulnerable, and I don't want you to get hurt."

Kate wanted to say, "Thank you, Ann Landers Schmidt. And what could you possibly know about 'loneliness of widowhood?'" Instead, she reminded herself that Kerrie had been a good friend for many years, and truly meant well.

"Kerrie, you are making a mountain out of a mole hill. Paul left today to go back to his home in Illinois. I have no idea when or if I'll see him again."

That seemed to reassure Kerrie, and much as she fought against it, Kate had to admit that once again, Kerrie was probably right.

Chapter Fifteen

Kate slept fitfully, tossing and turning all night long. At the sound of a dog barking, she awoke with a start and immediately sensed something was different. Her faithful bed partner, Amber, was not sleeping in any of his favorite spots on the bed.

She grabbed her robe from the bedpost and shuffled groggily down the hallway, checking the adjoining rooms and calling, "Amber, time for chunkies." This breakfast call should have brought her friend on the run, but instead produced nothing but silence.

With mounting concern, Kate extended her search to the lower level. As she crawled on hands and knees checking in the farthest recesses of the stair closet, Kate tried to convince herself this was only Amber's way of paying her back for leaving him alone most of yesterday. As a last resort she started to pull out the heavy hide-a-bed where Amber sometimes went to sulk, when something light caught her eye. It was Amber; still sound asleep, curled up in a ball on the open shelf of an old desk she planned to refinish.

"Amber, you frightened me! Why are you sleeping down here?" The cat yawned, stretched, and looked surprised with Kate's concern. As she lifted Amber up, the red spiral notebook he was sleeping on started to slip. Kate caught the book, and carried it upstairs along with Amber, depositing both a bit roughly on the island counter while she made coffee. When she turned around, Kate noticed Amber was again sprawled over the red notebook.

"OK, Amber, what's so fascinating about this ..." In mid-sentence she recognized a handwritten note taped to the front, "Letters to Ben – private." Opening the cover, she recognized the familiar salutation, and Opening – "I know you won't be reading this, but since it was your idea, I hope your ears twitch and your fingers burn every time I have to put my feelings on paper." She continued on until she had reread each entry, experiencing anew the emotions they had evoked. To her surprise, the catharsis felt good. Just why, she wasn't sure, but somehow she knew there was a reason. She stood quietly transfixed in thought, then slowly she was filled with a sense of excitement and discovery.

"Eureka," she whispered in Amber's ear. "Oh, Amber, you wonderful cat. I've been looking for someway to make sense out of my feelings, but there has been no one I could really talk to. Kerrie is the only person who even knows about Paul Dubois, and we know what she thinks I should do." Kate pulled the notebook out from under Amber's outstretched legs and held it up. "This was the answer once, and it just might help me again. Thank you, Amber. Thank you, Ben Gessler, and thanks be to God who works in mysterious ways, even through cats!" She kissed the top of Amber's head, and carried him with her to the dining room table. "Come on, cat. We've got some writing to do."

FEELINGS

Kate printed the letters large and bold like a heading across the paper, then giggled as she remembered Carol Burnett's delightful parody of that much overused audition song. She had grown comfortable using the letterform of journal writing, so she continued it now.

Dear Ben,

I had a lousy night of little sleep last night, and in part you are to blame. I was managing very well this past year keeping my emotional life tightly bottled up. I was all nice and numb before you pulled the plug. Now another doctor has entered my life, and I don't know what's happening – I'm afraid and angry, and wildly joyous, and out of control.

Reed certainly never sent me in those kinds of tailspins. Of course Reed came along when I needed another rudder in my life, a grounder, someone to steer me, keep me on course. I can't remember a time as I grew up that there wasn't a guide pole.

"You were a perfect child"-- my mother's words. From her perspective, I suppose I was. She directed, I followed. She had strong opinions. I had no opinions, or at least if they were different from my mother's, I suspected they were wrong.

Don't misunderstand. My mother wasn't an abuser, she was just – confident. Every club she belonged to – and there were many – sought her as president and spokesperson.

My father was such a quiet man, I rarely knew if he agreed or disagreed with my mother. He offered his opinion if I asked for it, but it was presented always as an option for me to consider, never as a commandment to be obeyed.

Just before I was married, however, I learned something about Daddy that explained why this marriage of opposites worked so well. I was packing my suitcase for the weekend honeymoon Reed and I had planned, and Mother was helping. As she held up a lacy negligee my sister had given me, her eyes sparkled, and she smiled a secret smile. "Kate, let me give you a bit of advice. Never tell Reed 'No' or 'I've got a headache.' Just give him a little time, and he'll change your mind." I knew from that revelation, that my sweet, soft-spoken Father had a passionate nature that more than satisfied his strong-willed wife.

With that strong will, she may have unconsciously controlled my decisions, but she in no way controlled my choice of interest. On that score she was an encourager. I loved to draw, so she provided the supplies. I loved to dance and act, so she provided ballet and dramatic art lessons. I had grandiose ideas of being on the stage, so she sent me to the University where I acquired an AB and MA in Theater Arts. I could entertain, but I couldn't manage practical matters.

Reed could and did. We met and fell in love while we both were earning our Masters. Reed was six years my senior, a returning World War II veteran, sobered by his years in combat. Evidently I was just the tonic he needed. I was hardly aware there had been a war. During my high school years I read the theater section of the paper and then was off to the Conservatory for lessons. The war carnage was a world apart from my life. I was attracted to Reed's mature and more serious nature. He, on the other hand, found my exuberance elevated his mood to a new plane.

For a while our paths separated. He went on a job search in Washington. I went to New York armed with letters of recommendations to Fred Friendly and other TV notables that I never got around to using. In order to pay the rent, I got a series of part time jobs requiring practical knowledge for which I was grossly under-qualified. I wrote of my plight to Reed. He came to New York, was hired by his business of choice, and we were married the same month.

Reed got a dreamy, disorganized ditz who couldn't confidently order food from a restaurant menu without first checking, "What are you going to have, Reed?" I got a sharp eyed pragmatist who lived on a time table and organized his socks and underwear drawer with the same precision that he managed his business. We should have driven each other crazy – and at times we did. The marriage lasted because we were the missing link that we both needed.

When Reed died, so did my steering mechanism. I had no one to charter my course. I managed with great difficulty to make the essential decisions, but had zero confidence. I went into hibernation, and would have stayed there if my friend, Kerrie, hadn't given me a verbal shot in the rear. That's when you and your sneaky "Feelings Journal" entered the picture, and shook me out of my emotional doldrums. I began to feel something again.

At the same time, my nerve endings returned. I felt a sense of "can do this" that I'd never felt before. I know I can manage my life. The decisions I make are OK, and so what if they aren't. They are mine, and I don't have to please anyone but myself.

So what's the problem? The problem is Paul Dubois. When I'm with — or even talk by phone to him — I feel like that ditzy, dreamy, no-can-do is trying to reappear again.

Kate sat for a long time thinking, then wrote a short sentence, underlined it, and closed the notebook. With a sudden burst of energy she had breakfast, got dressed, and called Martha. "Are you game for walking to the Village? I need to pick up my mail and get some milk." She looked toward the main cabin and added, "Let's walk the lake road. I see there is a west wind."

"How can you tell?" Martha asked.

"By the way the flag is blowing in my neighbor's yard."

"Your neighbor? Has the Hellman property been sold?"

Oops! Kate thought. Now Kerrie won't be the only person who knows about Paul Dubois.

"Yes, Martha. It was sold a little while ago. I'll tell you about it on our walk."

Chapter Sixteen

Kate was humming an off-key rendition of "I Could Have Danced All Night" as she charged in the front door after her walk to the Village. She stopped first at the thermostat before depositing a quart of milk in the refrigerator. Amber appeared from nowhere and stretched his declawed paws on the wood box.

"You're right, Amber. I think it's about time to crank up the wood stove." Kate made a face and sighed. "But first I suppose I'd

better get Kent to check the chimney flue, before I build the first fire of the season."

The wood stove was an alternative to their all-electric heating system. Kate and Reed used the stove more for its cheery, dry warmth, than its reduction of the fuel bill. Fire tending had been Reed's job, and that was just another thing Kate had had to learn to do.

Kate moved to the blue upholstered love seat with her mail, and Amber quickly jumped up beside her, "Look, Amber. A letter addressed to you." Amber looked interested. "I think there are some pictures in here of your new kitten cousins." He scratched his cheek on the edge of the envelope Kate was opening. Her daughter Jill had told Kate in their last phone conversation that the pictures were on the way. The new kittens were a kind of pet insurance. Their year old beagle, Hoss, was acutely deaf, nearly blind, and showing further signs of deterioration.

Three color photos lay displayed on Kate's lap and Amber sniffed them over. "There they are Amber. The handsome black one is Sassy, and those are his two tiger sisters, Andrea and Kissapher."

Amber put his creamy paw on the glossies, giving his stamp of approval. An enclosed, not printed on lined paper, said, "Dear Gramma Meow. Our kitties are getting big. Come see. We love you. Maureen."

Maureen had been begging Kate to come to their newly remodeled farm home, but Kate always had some excuse. Reed had always done the driving on that long trip, and it was just something else to try alone. "Why not?" a voice within her asked. "Yes, why not?" Kate answered aloud. Amber flinched at the sharpness of her voice.

Her walk with Martha had given Kate an ego boost. With Martha as her confidential sounding board, a weight had been lifted from her shoulders. In some respects, Martha was like Kate's father. As a non-judgmental listener, she heard Kate's problems and concerns over Paul Dubois' effect on her emotional life. Kate did not tell Martha about her physical attraction to Paul, but she did tell her about Kerrie's negative reaction, and the reactions she was sure she would get from her children and grandchildren. As they parted company this morning, Martha hugged Kate and whispered in her ear, "Put it in God's hands, Kate. He is the only judge in our lives."

Kate ate a large caramel apple for lunch, and started a "things-to-do" list. Number one was to check the car. Since Reed's death, she had relied on Bart's Mobile Station in town for the care and upkeep of her car. For a longer trip, she needed more car savvy.

Later that afternoon Kate's son Kent seemed surprised to find his mother parked beside the self service fuel tank at the Mobile station when he passed by on his way home from work.

"Mom! This is ridiculous. Even Dad never used self-service."

"That's true, but I may be doing a bit more traveling on the interstate, and it's something I should know how to do." She pointed to the fuel pump. "Just show me what to do and don't make a fuss."

When Kent started to protest, Kate wagged her finger in his direction. "Don't talk back to me, young man, or I'll cut off your supply of Special-K Bars." Begrudgingly, Kent went through the process and Kate took out a notebook.

"Now what are you doing?"

"I'm just taking a few notes so I won't forget."

"Mom!"

Kate had to smile. She knew her ineptness with anything mechanical drove her son up the wall. "What did they teach you in college anyway?" he liked to taunt.

Reed and Kate's children were exact opposites. Their daughter Jill was the bookworm, graduated valedictorian of her class, and went on to teach school.

Kent, who was just as intelligent, did only enough bookwork to get by. His great love was building. The three-story tree house he built on the clump of cedars down by the water when he was ten was the talk of the grade school. This tri-level wonder also included a trap door, screened porch, carpeting, and a dumb waiter system that defied description. Kent's high school shop instructor, Mr. Mathews, confided to Kate that Kent had the skill to teach that course by the time Kent was in tenth grade.

After high school, Kent worked for the Crystal Lake Construction Company until a job opened up at Strinberg's Power Company. Kent was married by then, so he took the course work required to get his electrician's license, and worked himself into a secure financial position for his growing family.

In the meantime, he built his own home by a little trout pond, and was Mr. Fixit for Reed and Kate whenever it was necessary.

This spurt of independence on his mother's part baffled Kent. Kate couldn't explain the force working within her either. But that force wouldn't be denied.

"I'll take you home, Kent, because I've a few more questions about my car." Courtney and Matthew were riding their bikes on their long gravel driveway, and both greeted Kate enthusiastically as she parked by their house.

"I got three books from the bookmobile today," Courtney said.

"Me, too!" echoed Matthew. "Wanna read them?"

"I'll read one apiece after your Daddy answers a few of my questions." Kate had her head down looking below the steering wheel as Kent opened her door.

"What are you looking for, Mom?"

"The hood thing-a-ma-jig. I've never really looked under the hood of the car, and my magazine here (Kate pointed to a recent issue of 'Car and

Driver') has a list of things I should check before taking any long trips."

"It's called a hood release, Mom. There it is to the left of the steering column."

Kate gave it a pull, expecting the hood to fly up. "Nothing happened!"

Kent moved to the front of the car. "There's a safety catch here under the front edge of the hood…"

"Wait," Kate interrupted. "Let me do it." Kate looked pleased when the hood lifted, then frowned as she surveyed the inner workings underneath.

"Want me to check your oil, Gramma?" Matthew asked in his best filling station attendant voice.

"Thank you very much, Matthew, but that's something I need to learn how to do." The group gathered around the car had now increased by one. Lynn, Kate's pretty, petite daughter-in-law, joined with a question of her own.

"Is Gramma having car trouble?"

Everyone had a comment, but Kate managed to get her answer heard over the rest. "I'm hoping to find out enough about what makes a car run to avoid trouble in the future." Kate pointed, "That looks like the dip-stick. How can I tell if I need some oil?"

"When was the last time you had your oil changed, Mom?"

"Oil changed?"

Kent looked at the passenger side doorframe and beckoned to Kate. "Every time you get your oil changed, which is about every three to four thousand miles, your service station attendant puts the information here. Dad must have had it changed the month before he died."

Kent looked at his Mother and smiled "You're right, Mom. You do need a refresher course on the care and upkeep of your car." He leaned over and opened the glove compartment and handed the Owners Manual to Kate. "Read this tonight. I'll be over tomorrow to see how much you learned."

Chapter Seventeen

After supper, Kate retired to the garage, and with her Sundance Owner's Manual propped on the steering wheel in front of her, scrunched down and carefully studied the pages, paying special attention to the "Maintenance" and "In Case of Emergency" sections. It was slow going.

As a teen, she had received her first driving instructions under the patient tutelage of her father. According to Reed, it hadn't been sufficient. "You're a road hazard, Kate. Indecisiveness doesn't work on the highway."

Reed made these observations after he and Kate – recently married and living in New York's Westchester County – had purchased their first car, and were out for their first ride on the thruway. To improve Kate's confidence, Reed took his newlywed out twice for personalized instruction. On the first outing, he was polite, but firm in his criticism. At the conclusion of the second lesson, Kate slammed the car door, the front door and the bedroom door with progressively increasing vigor, and remained incommunicado the rest of the evening.

The very next day Reed made arrangements for private driving lessons. Much to his surprise, after two weeks of instruction, Kate passed the New York written and driver's exam with higher marks than Reed. Only once did Reed make the mistake of insinuating that Kate may have done so by batting her baby blue eyes at the examiner.

The care and upkeep of the car had always been Reed's responsibility. Now Kent's insinuation that his mother didn't have the smarts to understand the Owner's Manual was all the motivation Kate needed.

When Kent arrived the following evening, he picked up the questioning where he left off the day before. "How often should you have the oil changed?"

"Every three or four thousand miles or three months," Kate fired back. "Check the oil filter every fifteen thousand miles."

Ten minutes later Kent stopped the questions, ran his hand through his black curly hair and asked incredulously, "Gosh, Mom, did you memorize the whole book?"

Kate beamed proudly, "It wasn't exactly fascinating reading, and I'm about thirty five years late getting the job done. I should have started reading owner's manuals fifteen cars ago."

Kate's mood changed. "Thanks, Kent, for your help, and thanks for checking the wood stove, filling the bird feeder, and so many other extras this past year." She put her hand on his shoulder.

Ken's deep blue eyes, so like his mother's, filled. He started to speak, but cleared his throat instead and headed toward the Special K Bars Kate had on the counter. With his mouth half-full he mumbled, "Why this interest in car maintenance all of a sudden?"

"I'm planning a trip to see Jill and the kids next week, if you, Courtney, and Matthew will feed Amber and the Outsiders for me."

"That's a five hour trip, Mom! I don't think Dad would..."

He stopped mid-sentence and Kate finished. "Mind, Kent? I don't think Dad would mind either."

That of course was not what Kent planned to say, but it's what Kate needed to feel.

Kent helped himself to more bars and moved over to the windows. "I heard the Hellman's sold their place. Have you heard who bought it?"

Kate felt her face flush, and chose her words carefully. "Dubois is the name."

"Young family?"

"Retired."

"Have you met them, Mom?"

"I've met Dr. Dubois. His grandchildren were visiting last week. I let them use our paddle boat."

Suddenly Kate saw a way to change the subject. "That reminds me, Kent. We've had some mighty cold nights lately. Before it gets too dark this evening, could you help me pull the paddleboat out of the water?

The paddleboat ploy worked, and for the next few minutes she and Kent dragged the boat up the ramp Reed had built on the end of the shored raft. Kate always hated this step in winterization because it meant the end of paddling with her grandchildren to see the eagle's nest at the mouth of the river.

Kate brought a bag of chocolate chip cookies from the freezer to the car. She knew Kent would have them eaten long before they were defrosted. He already had two cookies in his mouth as he waved goodbye.

The phone was ringing as Kate approached the back deck, and she was a bit winded by the time she picked up the receiver.

"Hi, Kate, this is Paul Dubois. I must have caught you outside."

At least, Kate thought, I have an excuse to sound breathless. "Oh, hello, Paul. You're right. I've been out with Kent putting the paddleboat in dry dock for the winter. Where are you calling from?"

"Hinsdale – arrived yesterday. I'd forgotten what a big cold place this is – and I'm not talking about the town. Speaking of homes, Kate, can you see my property from where you are?"

"Fairly well."

"How does the place look?"

"Still there. Hasn't moved an inch."

"Good!" Paul chuckled.

"But there have been a few changes since you left."

"Oh?" Paul's voice registered concern.

"Some strong winds shook down the last leaves from the big maple by the foot bridge last night. They make a lively splash of color on the still green grass underneath. The big birch by the guest house managed to hold on to most of its yellow leaves despite the big blow."

"Great! I can almost see it." There was an awkward pause and Paul added quickly. "I hope I'm not keeping you from anything."

Kate's flutter feeling had subsided and was replaced by a positive force of energy. "No. I was just making a list. I do that a lot. Always have. Maybe you can explain why I have that fetish, Doctor?"

"Well, Madame," Paul put on his doctor voice. "It depends on the kind of lists you make. If they are lists of dastardly deeds, people you plan to 'do in,' now THAT might be a problem."

"Oh, nothing so devilish, Doctor," Kate, responded quickly. "I'm planning a trip to visit my daughter in Middleton, and I don't want to forget anything. They've added three new members to their family, you know."

"Triplets?" Paul questioned with honest surprise.

Another long pause, and Kate filled it with a giggle. "Yes, triplets. Kitten triplets. A neighbor's cat, who is little more than a kitten herself, gave birth to a litter of five in Jill's garage."

"Hm, I see," Paul responded solemnly. "A classic case where early sex education might have helped."

"You got that right," Kate laughed. "And because the birth took place on their property, Jill's children claimed part ownership of the brood. I tried to tell Jill she has effectively added three more children to her home, but she laughed it off."

"Oh, I'm on Jill's side. I'd give anything to have my old cat, Casanova, with me right now."

Kate couldn't resist telling her maternal conscience, "See there, Mother, he likes cats -- so he can't be all bad."

But then Paul added, "How long do you expect to be away, Kate?" and Kate bristled. Why did Paul need to know anyway? Then she remembered she had agreed to keep an eye on his place.

"I'll probably be gone only a week. This will be the first time away from Amber, and I'm not sure how he'll react. I guess I'm foolish to even consider a cat's feelings. But..."

Paul interrupted, "No, Kate, I think you're quite right. Animals get lonely and depressed just like people. For a first time away, I'd say no longer than a week."

The vehemence of his reply surprised Kate. Again there was a pause. This time Paul continued. "I have a strange request, Kate. May I have Jill and Kent's addresses? Do they know I've purchased the Hellman's place?"

"I did mention your name to Kent today when he asked who bought the property. There has been no occasion to tell Jill."

Kate did think it an odd request, but gave Paul her children's addresses anyway before their phone conversation ended. She mentioned the unusual request to Martha when she called Kate just before bedtime. "Well, maybe he's a list-maker like you, Kate. And he's making a list of all those people who are – or may become – important in his life."

Thinking of those words later, she smiled and reached for Amber next to her on the bed. "Martha is such a good friend, Amber."

Chapter Eighteen

Despite all her advance preparation, when Kate jammed the last item into her car trunk the following morning, she felt Reed's disapproving presence.

Her husband had been a man of routine, and trips were his specialty. Reed kept Kate on a tight reign the day before a trip was scheduled. Kate met his departure time only with constant prompting from Reed. "Have you laid out the clothes you plan to wear? What time should I set the alarm so you have time to pack the cosmetic case?"

Reed didn't blow a whistle like Captain Von Trapp. Had he done so, Kate told Reed once when they were watching "The Sound of Music" together, she would have pushed the offending mouthpiece up his nose, or worse. Still, he got the same desired effect by standing at the front door checking his watch at frequent intervals. Once in the car, Kate was allowed only two trips back in the house to get a forgotten item before Reed's patience was unalterably "tried."

Kate shook her head. Reed would certainly not be happy with the fact that this morning she was leaving a full hour later than planned. "It's OK, Mom," Jill assured Kate when she called her daughter, and was breathlessly reciting the reasons for her delay. "Just drive carefully."

Jill was like her father in many ways - even looked like the Stenson side of the family. But once she became a mother herself, Jill was more sympathetic to Kate's innate disorganization. Motherhood had not come easily for Jill. Her doctor explained that endometriosis had essentially closed her fallopian tubes. Finally, after ten childless years, Jill and Keith adopted Maureen, a beautiful, black-eyed baby from New Delhi, India. Three years later William was born, confounding the doctors who had told Jill it was impossible. Her miracle children now filled Jill's life, and took precedence over everything else, including missed schedules.

Kate's trip to Middleton was uneventful, but tiring. She was relieved when she finally pulled in the long, winding driveway of the old farmhouse Jill and Keith were renovating.

Near the house she could see activity. William was in a monstrous sandbox filled with trucks and other sand moving equipment. Maureen was hanging upside down on the jungle gym swing. The children apparently didn't see Kate at first, but once she was spotted, their shouting alerted Jill, who came from the house and joined in the noisy greeting. Their old Beagle, Hoss, barked his "hellos" with such force he had to be taken back in the house before the car unloading started.

Kate opened the trunk and laughed. "I know it looks like I've come for a month, but Lynn sent several bags of her kids' hand-me-downs for William and Maureen. The boots and winter jackets are mine in case fall turns into winter while I'm here.

"What are these, Gramma Meow?" Maureen had spotted several bags with wrapped packages inside.

"Presents!" shrieked William.

"Let's wait till we get Gramma's things inside," instructed Jill. "Maureen, you be the door opener, and William watch that the kittens don't get out."

"Oh, my, yes!" Kate exclaimed. "I can't wait to see those kittens. I have presents for them, too." The furry triplets who had been watching from the entrance hall window ledge, proved to be even cuter than their photographs.

"What did you get the kittens, Gramma?" William whispered settling his small rump on Kate's knee and circling one arm around her neck.

"Let's find out, shall we? Maureen, see those three paper sacks next to my tote bag? Lay them on their sides on the floor please."

Maureen did as she was told, and within minutes, Sassy, the all-black male of the trio, approached and cautiously put his nose in one of the partially opened sacks. Andrea and Kissifer watched their bolder brother briefly, then they too started investigating. Before long each kitten had disappeared into the paper confines. Like sack-enclosed jumping beans, the kitten-filled parcels popped over the floor.

"What are they playing with inside?" Maureen wanted to know.

"Catnip filled mice, among other things." Kate dug deeper into her tote bag and extracted a woven basket, "Amber has a basket like this one filled with his play things. He goes to it at night, and I see two or three different cat toys at the foot of my bed in the morning."

Kitten play was a fun-filled beginning to a beautiful week for Kate. The day before she was scheduled to leave, however, something happened that might have marred her stay, had she let it.

The morning had been spent at various rummage sales. Kate bought a Ninja Turtle outfit for William and several dress-up clothes to add to Maureen's "let's pretend" trunk. The afternoon was sunny, so Jill and Kate sat outside watching the children play. Three-year-old William climbed to the top of the slide, encased in his green Ninja Turtle jump suit, and let out a whoop, pointing his sword at an imaginary foe below. His turtle mask partially covered his fair skin, and the red cape fluttered in the breeze as he slid down the mountain to engage in a fight to the death.

"I hope this violent stage ends soon," Jill sighed. "William and I have talked it over, and he assures me, 'I only kill the bad guys, Mommy'."

Kate smiled and shook her head, "This too shall pass. In my time it was cops and robbers and cowboys and Indians."

While William fought off the evildoers, Maureen moved to a different tune. She had chosen rainbow colored dance wear from her costume box, and layers of silk and chiffon swished and swirled with her every twist and turn.

Maureen had been unusually quiet and neither her mother nor grandmother could figure out why. Suddenly Maureen stopped dancing and moved toward Kate. She looked like an exotic bird. Her thick, waist-length black hair was drawn up to the top of her head and held in place with a hot-pink ribbon. Her softly curled bangs accented her black eyes, usually sparkling with joy, but today sad and brooding. Kate took hold of Maureen's hands and pulled her closer, "What's the matter, Maureen?"

"I hate Papa Stenson," she lashed out angrily. Jill looked shocked and started to speak, but Kate shook her head to stop her. Gathering Maureen in her arms, she asked softly, "Why are you angry with Papa, Maureen?"

Sobs came now. "Be -be – cause he – he left us – and I can't play with him anymore." Kate rested her head on her granddaughter's quaking shoulders and let her own tears fall. She was unaware that Jill had left until she returned with a box of Kleenex, her own eyes red from weeping.

For a while Kate just held Maureen close, swaying ever so slightly. The gentle rocking motion seemed to ease Maureen's pain. When the sobs had ceased, Kate spoke quietly, "Do you know what Gramma does when she gets lonely for Papa?" Maureen shook her head, still buried in Kate's bosom. "I ask God for help."

Maureen raised her head slowly to look into Kate's eyes. "What does God tell you, Gramma?"

"He shows me where to look to feel close to Papa."

Maureen's surprised expression demanded further explanation. Kate continued. "God shows me the hanging lamp in the dining room and I laugh remembering how Papa and I practically hung by our toenails trying to get the lamp straight." A trace of a smile flickered across Maureen's mouth. "God shows me the chiming clock in the stairwell, and I remember how Papa had me stand on the stairs with the clock shelf resting like a hat on my head, until we found just the right spot on the wall to place it." That image elicited a giggle.

"And then God shows me the blue recliner where Papa often sat with you on his knee going 'toot – toot – toot.'" With each "toot" Kate's knee flipped Maureen higher, until a full-blown laugh erupted.

Kate noticed that William had been unaware of the scene being acted out between Maureen and herself, and she was glad. After all, William had been a mere toddler when Reed died, and his memory of his Grandfather Stenson was probably quite dim.

Jill had also moved away. As soon as she saw that Kate had Maureen pacified, she had walked down the driveway to pick up the mail. She was frowning a bit when she returned.

"You got a letter, Mom, from somebody in Hinsdale, Illinois." She squinted at the return address. "It's hard to read the writing, but it looks like Paul Dubois. Who is he?"

Kate wanted to tell Jill the whole story, but with Maureen and William close by she decided to wait till later. She put the letter into her jacket pocket and said, "The Dubois bought the Hellman's property. Their year round home is in Hinsdale."

Later that evening, while Jill was putting Maureen and William to bed, Kate kicked off her shoes and curled up on the sofa to read Paul's letter. When she opened the envelope, a photograph fell in her lap. The subject was a handsome sandy-haired cat sitting on the hood of a car. Printed on the back were the words, "Casanova Dubois – 1985". Eagerly, Kate opened the letter. It was handwritten and surprisingly legible for a doctor, Kate noted.

"Dear Kate,

"I've been going through some family albums today, and came across this portrait of a good friend of mine. My daughter Ann tells me that Casanova bears a strong resemblance to your Amber. What do you think?

"I first made "C's" acquaintance one hot summer evening as I left home for the hospital. I had parked the car in our driveway, and left the windows open. When I opened the car door and sat down, a huge Tomcat jumped from the back into the passenger seat with a look on his face that seemed to say "OK. Let's get moving." Although I'd never actually seen this cat before, I had seen many of his look-alike offspring. This amorous vagabond had a reputation for wooing every feline female within seven states– isn't that how you Hoosiers put it?

"Mom?" Startled, Kate looked up to find Jill sitting on the sofa beside her. "I'm sorry to interrupt you, but Maureen wanted you to know that God showed her Papa tonight." Tears came to Kate's eyes as Jill continued her explanation. "We read a bedtime story Papa gave to her – now go ahead and finish your letter."

"No, I'll finish it later. I'd rather talk to you."

"When did you meet the Dubois family?"

"Well, I've only met Mr. – that is Dr. Dubois and his daughter, Ann."

"Oh? Where was Mrs. Dubois?"

At this point Kate thought she'd better start the story at the beginning.

She was selective in her narration, and did not mention the lunch date. Still she was a little surprised by Jill's reaction. "Now he's writing you letters? I'd be careful, Mom. You're a very attractive lady. Don't let this Dr. Dubois take advantage of your kind nature."

Kate lay awake a long time that night. She kept going over the reactions of her best friend, Kerrie, and now Jill, to Paul Dubois. She knew both of them only wanted the best for her, but somehow Kate felt hurt and a bit angry. Neither of them asked how she felt. Shouldn't that be important, too?

Chapter Nineteen

As Kate's anger accelerated, so did her speed. Suddenly she noticed flashing red lights in the south bound lane. "Slow down, Lady," she warned herself, and put on the cruise control. That left only her emotions and appetite in high gear. Kate had stopped at a wayside earlier to eat the sandwich and fruit she had brought from Jill's, but it hadn't satisfied her hunger. When she saw a high rise sign advertising a restaurant known for its superlative baked goods, she turned off the interstate at the next exit.

Once inside the eatery, Kate leaned her forehead against the bakery display case, ogling the lushly iced cupcakes, cream filled éclairs, and tempting pies. The waitress arrived almost the minute she was seated, and rather than bother with decisions, Kate ordered a mile-high-lemon pie and coffee to eat here and half dozen chocolate cupcakes and a dozen peanut butter cookies 'to go.'

For the past month Kate had managed to curb this kind of gluttony, and now she blamed this fall off the diet wagon on her emotional state. As she waited for the food to arrive, she searched in her purse for Paul's letter. Smoothing the wrinkled envelope, Kate ran her hands over her name, written in Paul's bold black script, receiving a sense of comfort from the act. "Why" she thought, "did both Jill and Kerrie find Paul Dubois a threat to her life? Paul's daughter, Ann, didn't appear to feel that way. How had Ann put it on the day she returned the cookie canister, 'Thanks for being a friend for Dad...' Of course, neither Kerrie nor Jill had actually met Paul."

Kate smiled as she looked once again at the photo of Paul's cat, Casanova, and continued reading from the point Jill interrupted her the night before.

"How are the kitten's triplets reacting to their grandmother's visit? Growing up on the farm meant raising numerous cat families. Every spring I had several litters to name and watch grow.

"Ann is coming next weekend for a short visit. The last day of her stay in Lake Crystal she surprised me with the comment, 'Dad, why do you keep the Hinsdale Place? It's so big for one person. It's full of memories, many of which I'd like to forget.' You know, Kate, I've felt the same way for two years, but Ann grew up in the Hinsdale home,

and I've kept it primarily for her sake. We could have saved each other a lot of pain had we been more honest with each other from the beginning."

Paul's last sentence was more of a balm for Kate's mood, than the calorie laden lemon pie that followed. "As soon as I get home, I must send Paul a photograph of kitten's triplets," she thought, "along with some honest feelings of my own."

However, several events followed Kate's return to Lake Crystal that put most thoughts of Paul Dubois aside. Courtney's teacher, Gail Shannon, called with a surprise request the evening Kate returned. Gail was program chairman of a regional workshop for kindergarten through third grade teachers featuring the art of story telling. Through Mrs. Shannon, word of Kate's popularity with Courtney's classmates in this art form had reached other teachers in the area, and those teachers had requested Kate as their featured speaker.

At first Kate refused. The more Gail insisted, the more Kate thought, "Why not! I've certainly told enough stories to my grandchildren and church school classes. There are any number of textbooks written on the subject. It might just be fun." She had three weeks to get her act together.

Martha also called soon after Kate's return to talk about the Christmas musical, which was now scheduled for the first week of December. Things seemed to be moving almost too smoothly in that department. The cast members with speaking parts had learned their lines, and the church choir was well on its way to mastering the songs.

Kate had been home barely a week when an early blast of winter arrived, delivering eight inches of snow to Lake Crystal.

When Kate and Reed were both working, an overnight snow of this depth meant quickly shoveling the garage door clear. It was the kind of labor they both enjoyed. Winter was one of the reasons they chose to move to northern Wisconsin. Up here people knew winter was coming, dressed for the cold, then got out and enjoyed the season's activities.

This Saturday morning following the snowfall, Kate and Amber dawdled over breakfast, absorbing the transformed scene before them. The still open lake reflected the pink tint of the morning sky. Enough sun slipped through the lake mist to pencil shadows of the hardwood and hemlock trunks on the soft mounds of snow. Kate picked up Amber and moved closer to the windows. Despite the snow's depth, Kate could see cat tracks leading to the Evergreen Mall on the far side of the creek bed. Amber's ears perked as he watched Blackie's dark form leap through the drifts and disappear under the snow laden balsam boughs. Kate nuzzled her pet. "It looks like good shopping at the Mall today." Amber licked his lips and swallowed, possibly weighing the pros and cons of being an inside cat.

Snow also meant sliding. After Kate finished shoveling, she issued a sliding party invitation to the grandchildren that they enthusiastically accepted. As soon as the roads were plowed, Mathhew and Courtney arrived. All but their bright eyes were encased in snowsuits, boots, caps, scarves and mittens.

"It's my turn to go first, Gramma," Mathhew said. Kate nodded, remembering her promise. Courtney had been granted the trial run the previous year. Her young grandson surveyed the sled course from the top of the hill. "Gramma, was that tree there last year?" he asked, pointing to a four-foot willow near the creek bed.

"Last year it was more like a bush. I'd stay on this side of the tree, Matthew, or your first trip down will be a wet one." Her grandson did as directed, and the red plastic toboggan skimmed over the snow at top speed, stopping twenty-five feet from the lake's edge. At that point, the tall dried stems of loosestrife, reed grass, and cattails were a natural barrier to further travel. As he trudged up the hill through the deep snow, Matthew's proud smile signaled his appreciation of Kate's trust.

"I'm next, Gramma. Give me a push," Courtney demanded. Even with that assistance, her added weight slowed her speed, making Matthew the distance winner. Such a loss a year ago would have reduced Courtney to tears. But today, with several months of kindergarten give and take under her belt, she reacted quite differently. With a giggle, she rolled from the toboggan onto her back, making a snow angel with her arms before heading up the hill again.

"Now it's your turn, Gramma," both kids chorused. Kate adjusted her earmuffs and positioned herself at the highest point of the slope.

"Who's going to give me a push?"

That's all Matthew and Courtney needed to hear. With a running start, both grandchildren pushed Kate halfway down the hill. This added momentum sent her sailing over a snowdrift and off course to within inches of the creek bank. Kate yelped and rolled off just seconds before the toboggan slid into the water. Their grandmother's plight sent Courtney and Matthew rolling down the hill like snowballs to her rescue. After that the toboggans were forgotten. Matthew and Courtney spent the rest of the time seat down or "butt" sliding as they called it.

Later, while the wet clothes were being dried, Kate served her guests hot chocolate mounded high with melted marshmallows. The kids insisted that Amber join their party, so he jumped up in Reed's chair, a silent observer of their fun.

Martha called the next day with another kind of snow report. "The cross country ski trails have been groomed. Are you game, Kate?"

The County Forestry Department, which was headquartered in Lake Crystal, managed two hundred and sixty acres of forestland in the country, and also groomed ten miles of cross-country trails overlooking the river valley just south of town.

Martha had introduced Kate to this sport last January saying she desperately needed a skiing companion. It was Kate who was desperate – desperate for something to fill the void Reed's death had left in her life.

"It helps to have a sense of humor when you're learning this sport," Martha explained on their first outing. Kate was proving to be an exceptionally gifted student until she attempted to turn around and executed a Chaplinesque pratfall into a snow bank.

"Oops!" giggled Martha, as she hastily dug her friend out of the tangle of snow, skis and ski poles. "I forgot to mention that the important thing to remember when turning is that your feet – rather your skis--are six feet long."

With last year's experience behind her, today Kate felt relaxed and comfortable with her equipment as she snapped on her skis in the parking lot. "I think I'm ready for the 'Big Hill,'" Kate announced to Martha, as they started the two-mile loop.

"Living dangerously these days are we?" Martha asked.

"Nothing ventured, nothing gained," Kate replied with a quirky grin.

There were quite a few small slopes on the two-mile loop. But the "Big Hill" that Kate referred to was especially steep and had an abrupt turn at the bottom. When they reached the spot in question, Martha waited at the top while Kate began her slow descent. About midway down, Kate's speed increased and her confidence wavered briefly. Then a new resolve kicked in, and her fear changed to joy as she made the turn at the bottom.

For the next few weeks Kate's life would resemble the challenge of the "Big Hill."

AMBER KNOWS BEST

Chapter Twenty

"Thanks a lot, Amber!"

Amber was not in sight, but his activities from the night before were quite evident. Kate had left her material for the story telling workshop spread out on the dining room table, which must have mightily pleased her playful puss. Papers, pens, and pencils, paper clips, felt tip markers, and even a heavy anthology that must have been close to the table edge, were scattered under the table and beyond.

The surge of creative energy, which had fueled Kate's late night writing activity, was at a low ebb this morning. As she waited for the coffee to brew, Kate watched a flock of male Evening Grosbeaks descend into the feeder, successfully scaring away the nuthatches and chickadees that had been peacefully breakfasting together before the large, chunky finches arrived. They scattered hulls as they ate, fighting amongst themselves over the choicest sunflower seeds.

"Gluttons!" Kate muttered to herself. It wasn't that she wanted to deny these vivid black, yellow, and white creatures their repast; it was their wasteful habits she'd like to change. Had their feeder been hung in the ordinary manner, it would not have been a problem. It wasn't. The bird feeder was suspended on a two-by-four, eight feet from the screen porch overhang.

"How on earth do you fill it?" Kate's sister, Jeanine, asked on her first visit to Lake Crystal.

"It's not easy," Kate responded with a sigh.

"Then why don't you put it closer?"

Reed, who had joined the sisters on the porch for some molasses cookies and iced tea, laughed at that innocent question. "Go ahead, Kate, tell your sister just why it isn't closer." Jeanine turned to catch her sister's grimace.

"OK," Kate shook her head. "You asked for it. It all has to do with squirrels and their dispositions. At least the squirrels here in Lake Crystal.

I can't remember seeing two gray squirrels that could stand each other. I'm glad I don't understand their chattering. Their body language is explicit enough to make me blush."

Jeanine laughed. "I still don't see what this has to do with bird feeders."

"We didn't either. At first Reed and I found it amusing to watch this character quirk in action. It was great sport to sit here and observe what happened when the second gray squirrel arrived at the feeder. If a few choice squirrel invectives did not deter the intruder, the chase was on," Kate pointed as she relived the scene. "Squirrel #1 would chase squirrel #2 off the feeder, onto that plum tree, into and up the blue spruce and over to the white birch. At that point we would lose sight of the actors and could follow the action only by the sight of jerking branches as the chaser and chasee would leap from bough to bough, tree to tree, and off into the woods."

As if on cue, a squirrel jumped from the blue spruce Kate had mentioned, and onto the deck railing looking for any kind of food morsels he could find.

Kate continued her story, "It slowly became apparent that the squirrels were eating more than their due. This was, after all, a 'bird' feeder we had purchased. I should explain that it wasn't THAT feeder." Kate gestured to the present feeder, now being inhabited by a pair of Red-Winged Blackbirds.

"Our original feeder was cylindrically shaped with a metal tray at the bottom to accommodate the larger birds. That feeder was hung under the eaves and easily accessible from the deck – too easily.

After the squirrels had eaten the contents from the bottom tray, they suspended themselves upside-down from the top of the feeder and ate from the smaller openings." Kate turned to Jeanine and smiled with clenched teeth. "But those openings were evidently too small for their satisfaction, so they increased the hole size by gnawing the plastic around the metal, causing the feed to spill out continuously."

"Why those little dickens!" Jeanine gasped.

"Our feelings exactly," Kate agreed. "That little trick proved too much even for our generous natures. Reed and I decided we would sprinkle enough seed on the deck to satisfy the squirrels, and get a new feeder – one that the squirrels could not use."

"Do they make that variety?" Jeanine asked.

Kate and Reed gave each other a knowing glance, and Kate continued, "Oh, yes. We found there were any number of bird feeders on the market that promised to be 'squirrel proof.' After comparing the merits of each, we decided to go 'top of the line.' We'd get the most expensive variety with a slick plastic dome."

"The one you have now?"

Kate continued without answering her sister. "I can remember our sense of satisfaction. Can't you, Reed?'

Reed nodded with a twinkle in his eye that led Jeanine to anticipate more trouble ahead. She turned back to Kate, who was obviously relishing telling the rerun.

"Gleefully, we assembled our new contraption, hung it from a two by four that extended several feet from our screened porch, and sat back to enjoy the birds, who could now eat without interruption." Jeanine opened her mouth, but before she could comment, Kate continued her monologue.

"What we didn't know was that while Mother Squirrel may not have taught her youngsters the virtue of sharing, she did teach them the virtue of risk taking – and risks they took. They tried jumping from the plum tree and missed. They tried jumping from the deck railing and missed. They tried jumping from the porch roof and missed. They even tried hanging upside down by their toe nails and sliding down the dome covering-- and missed, diving headfirst twenty-five feet to the ground below."

"Oh, no!" Jeanine laughed, opening the screen door to peer over the deck railing. "That's a long way down."

Kate poured her audience more tea, and continued her story telling. "Like you, we laughed, and felt smug, and went on about our business-- until two days later I looked out the kitchen window and saw a gray squirrel IN OUR FEEDER."

"No!" shouted Jeanine.

"YES!" echoed Kate. "And of course, since one of their kind made it, the others confidently followed his example.

"We were incensed, of course. That feeder was expensive. <u>Birdfood</u> was expensive. We felt there had to be a simple answer to this dilemma. There was an answer all right, but it wasn't so simple. It was man versus beast, and believe you me, Jeanine, for a while it looked like the latter would prove the victor.

"First we watched those acrobats to see how they managed to defy gravity. When we saw they were leaping from the plum tree, we cut off every accessible branch. When we could see they were leaping from the deck railing, we extended the two-by-four a bit farther. Of course, the farther out the feeder was placed, the harder it became to retrieve it for replenishing the seeds. But that was no longer a consideration. Now it was a matter of our reputation. Our friends were beginning to ask us with a smile, 'Are you still feeding the squirrels?'"

"Are you still feeding the squirrels?" Jeanine asked.

Kate gave her sister a toothy grin. "I'm pleased to report that we no longer have squirrels in our feeder. However, as you can plainly see, we do have a pitifully one-sided plum tree, a bird feeder that has been extended so far it is almost impossible to refill, and a new-found respect for gray squirrels."

The click of the coffee maker and the inviting aroma of the fresh brew brought Kate back to the present. As Kate watched the grosbeaks scatter seed, she wrote "Refill feeder" on the refrigerator reminder pad. That was something Kent had to do because it required unhooking the heavy dome topped feeder with a nine-foot pole. Until recently, Kate hadn't minded making that request. Now she did. She could manage the bills, the car, the wood stove. There must be some way she could manage that feeder.

Chapter Twenty-One

At 9:15, just as the phone rang, Kate glanced at her watch.

"Hi, Mrs. Stenson." Kate recognized the pleasant lilt of Gail Shannon's voice even before she identified herself. "I've cleared things with the office to have the video camera equipment in my classroom by 10:30. My aide will do the filming. Oh, by the way, yesterday the kids selected your granddaughter, Courtney, to be the first storyteller."

"Oh, yes? Well Courtney is certainly used to being on camera. Her parents have every major and minor step of her life on video tape."

"Good. I know some children would be camera-shy. I certainly like the idea of using this video for the workshop. Kids are natural storytellers. Unfortunately, once we start teaching reading, the storytelling gets dropped from the curriculum. Maybe your workshop will change that."

Speed was never Kate's forte, but it was necessary this morning. As she crawled around the floor collecting her materials to take to the elementary school, she had some unkind thoughts for the cat that had caused this delay. Amber was still out of sight. As she passed the food dish, she noticed he had not eaten much, if anything, the night before, which was unusual. Kate had little time to speculate on this sudden show of abstinence. "He was probably too tuckered out playing table hockey with my writing supplies," Kate grumbled under her breath.

Courtney and her classmates were just coming in from recess when Kate arrived. Several children asked Kate if she would be telling them stories today. She was noncommittal until all were in their seats. "This morning I'm not the storyteller. I've come to enjoy listening to you. Mrs. Shannon tells me Courtney will be first. Where would you like us to sit, Courtney?"

Courtney looked pleased to be in charge. "Over there." She pointed to a carpeted area free of chairs where Mrs. Shannon often read to the class. It was ideal for videotaping, because the children would be at a lower level and the camera could be moved around easily, catching both Courtney's expressions and those of her listeners.

"What story would you like to tell us today, Courtney?" Kate asked as

Courtney's classmates settled themselves on the floor.

"The story of Peter Rabbit."

Kate knew Courtney had just received the Beatrix Potter collection, and a stuffed Peter look-a-like for her birthday, so she wasn't surprised with this choice. What did surprise Kate, however, was the ease with which Courtney selected the dramatic moments of the plot, and the voices, to indicate the various characters. It was easy to tell who was speaking—Mr. McGregor, Peter, or the other animals in the story.

Courtney's peers were an appreciative audience. They laughed at Peter's stint in the watering can, and his other misadventures. Kate had a "how to" list for the adult workshop. She discovered today that this was not a prerequisite for young storytellers.

"Can I be next?" Bo, a freckled redhead jumped up wildly waving his hand. Rule number five on Kate's list read: "Rehearse story aloud simply, but with energy. Have fun." Bo did not need a rehearsal. Bo, in fact, had so much energy and so much fun telling "The Three Little Pigs" that Mrs. Shannon had to employ the old vaudeville hook to get him off stage. The "hook" in this case was the promise that Bo could tell another of his favorite stories some day very soon.

After a brief conference with Mrs. Shannon, firming the details of next week's workshop, Kate picked up the video, and stopped by the post office before heading home. As was her custom, she quickly sorted through the junk stuff and deposited it into the already full waste can for that purpose. In so doing, she almost missed the letter caught between the pages of a grocery ad. She pulled it out and felt a surge of joy when she recognized Paul Dubois' bold, black handwriting. Outside of the post office, in the privacy of her car, Kate read Paul's letter.

Dear Kate,

When your letter arrived yesterday, I opened it with the same happy anticipation I used to feel as a youngster back on the farm when my birthday card arrived from Aunt Maude. Maude was Grandfather Dubois' maiden sister who taught elementary school for fifty years. Aunt Maude gave my brother Bob and me $10 every year on our birthdays.

Please tell your daughter I greatly appreciated the photograph she took of the kitten triplets being held by their Grandmother Stenson. I have it on the desk here beside me, and look at it often as I write.

Ann's visit was a good one. I'm glad she didn't bring the boys this time because it gave us the opportunity to talk father-to-daughter in a way we've never done before. We talked openly about the good and not so good parts of our relationship.

You can't go back, but I wish now Sue and I had provided a sister or brother for Ann. I hadn't realized the pressure and responsibility an only child feels. I know now how insensitive I was to Ann's feelings during Sue's illness and death. Siblings can share family problems. Not perfectly, perhaps, but the support is there. I hated to see Ann leave. At least we've opened the door to a more honest communication.

So, there is enough snow in Lake Crystal for winter recreation. I'm trying to imagine what my place looks like with a snow cover. No, I have never tried cross-country skiing, but I'd like to learn. Sue and I vacationed in Aspen several times with the Walkers, and I managed downhill OK.

Your life seems very full. Mine is not. I've never been much of a joiner. My excuse was always my "on call" status as a surgeon. I still get a certain number of social invitations as the obligatory single male. I can only feel sorry for the obligatory single female who is provided to keep me company.

I'm glad I have a friend like you who will listen and hopefully understand my situation.

My best to Amber and the Outsiders.

Paul

Kate sat for a while thinking about what Paul had written. "I've never been much of a joiner." She couldn't be sure of Paul's spiritual life, and it wasn't her right to judge. She was grateful for the strength she received from her church family, and remembered the day Reed died. Martha arrived at her door holding a coffee cake. Kate wasn't aware of the food until much later. Martha stepped inside the door and reached for Kate.

They said nothing. They just held each other. "Paul must have that kind of friend in Jerry Walker," Kate thought. She shivered then, and realized how cold the car had become. The noon fire whistle explained her hunger. She had only a small dish of cereal before leaving for school that morning.

When Kate opened the front door, her buoyant mood changed. She sensed something was wrong when Amber was not at his customary spot by the stairs to greet her. His food had not been touched, another ominous sign. She dropped her storytelling material and mail on the island counter and ran downstairs. Sometimes Amber slept in sun on the wool afghan that covered the stagecoach bed. The bed was empty. "Amber!" Kate called loudly as she ran back upstairs. She heard something in response. It wasn't a "meow," but more like a primal scream from an animal in acute pain. The sound was coming from the laundry room where Amber's litter box was kept. Kate found him there, straining and writhing in agony.

Chapter Twenty-Two

Kate's hand trembled as she dialed Dr. Scheer's number. "Please, please be there," she begged pacing back and forth, twisting the retractable cord with her free hand. After five rings, the answering service clicked on. "This is Dr. Joanne Scheer. Please leave a message and your phone number and I will return your call as soon as possible."

"Oh, no!" Kate moaned, very aware that meant the veterinarian could be anywhere in the two-county area where she performed her small animal practice. When the beep sounded, Kate tried to control her panic and collect her thoughts. "This is Kate Stenson calling. We have an emergency. Our nine-year-old cat Amber is in extreme pain. He keeps straining in the litter box with no results. Our number is 555-4993.

Amber's anguished cry immediately propelled Kate to the laundry room. "Here I am, Amber." Kate reached out, but her gentle touch brought no glimmer of recognition from her deranged pet.

Fear gripped Kate. She recalled how she felt when their last cat, Toby, died. At that time there was little to be done to prevent feline leukemia and Reed and Kate grieved together after tests determined their thirteen-year-old angora had contracted that fatal disease. After Toby's death, Kate had stated unequivocally, "I never want another cat!" Of course that was before she met Amber.

The first cat funeral Kate remembered was that of Kitty Lindy--named after the famed aviator. Kate was five and was saddened by the car accident that caused his untimely death. Her sister Jeanine was ten at the time, and she was devastated--not so much by his death-- but by the fact her girl friend had told her the day after the funeral that since cats don't have souls, they can't go to heaven. Jeanine tearfully brought this information to the dinner table. Kate smiled now as she remembered how her father handled this disturbing bit of news. "Jeanine, do you think you will need Kitty Lindy when you go to Heaven?" Jeanine had vigorously nodded her tear-streaked face. "Then Kitty Lindy will be there. God has promised us that in heaven we will have everything we need."

As Kate watched her ailing pet now she remembered the reason Amber became a part of her family--despite her misgivings. Amber had come mewing at Kent's door one frigid night. The temperature was thirty degrees below zero, and the cat was bedraggled and emaciated. Her son's family already included a cat, a dog and two young children, but they took in Amber, cleaned and fattened him, and had him neutered and declawed. When Lynn found his shedding white hair to be just too much extra work, Kent asked Kate and Reed to take him for a "trial run." Kent knew Amber would ingratiate himself into his parents' heart after the first day. Of course he was right.

The phone jarred Kate back to the present. "Oh, please make it be Dr. Scheer."

"Hello. This is Dr. Scheer." Kate breathed a sigh of relief.

"I got your message about Amber."

"Thank you, Dr. Scheer. He is in so much pain. What do you think is the matter?"

"From your description, I think Amber has a bladder stone, but I need a little more information. First we must find out if the urethra is completely blocked."

"How do I do that?" Kate questioned.

"I want you to find the bladder. It is located in the lower abdomen."

"What does it feel like?"

"For a cat Amber's weight, it will be the size of a lime or lemon."

"Oh dear! Amber is in so much pain now. Will this hurt him more?"

"It probably will, but it's necessary."

Kate did as she was told, but when she found the bladder, Amber shrieked and struggled to get away. "Dr. Scheer," the tears were beginning to come now, "I found the bladder, but when I touched it, he got away from me."

"Was it hard or soft?"

"Very hard, and he looks--I don't know. His eyes look so different--sunken and strange."

"He is probably dehydrated, and that's not a good sign."

Kate's tear flowed freely now. "Oh, Dr. Scheer, what can I do?"

"Just try not to worry, Kate. Amber's condition is very treatable, and I think we have caught it in time. I've finished with my last appointment and I'm about a half-hour away. See you very soon."

That half hour was an eternity to Kate. When Dr. Scheer finally arrived, she detailed the procedures she would be using at her clinic--the catheter to release the urine, intravenous liquids to correct and prevent further dehydration, and a urinalysis to check for bacteria and blood in the urine. She explained it was important to know the type of stone or crystals before she prescribed medication.

Kate could hardly bear to watch as Dr. Scheer put the reluctant Amber into the Pet Taxi. "I will perform the surgery as soon as I get to the clinic, Kate, and call you in a couple of hours with the results."

"When will I be able to bring him home?"

"Two days should be sufficient. By then he should be eating. Depending on the results of the tests, I'll know what kind of diet to prescribe."

"Diet! Oh, no!" Kate moaned, remembering Amber's refusal to eat anything other than his favorite bill-of-fare."

As Dr. Scheer got into her van, she assured Kate, "There are a variety of brands to choose from--some even my most finicky patients like." With a wave, she quickly drove off.

Kate leaned weakly against the garage door, drained from the emotional trauma of the last hour. In the past, when a member of her family was seriously ill, she would call the church prayer chain. Kate certainly considered Amber a member of her family, but she couldn't request prayer for a CAT. "I'll call Lynn and Jill," she thought. "They would want to know."

The house was empty and quiet. On her way to the wall phone, Kate tripped over Amber's toy basket. This evidence of her pet's recent healthy habits brought tears again. She reached down to pick up the balls, catnip mouse, and other cat curios, then fell to her knees and prayed, "Dear God, I know you love and care for all your earthly creatures. Please, be with Amber, Dr. Scheer--and all the other families who have pets in need of your healing power."

Kate knew then the peace she always felt when she shared her problems with the source of her strength. She also felt better when she talked to Lynn and Jill. Since Amber had lived with Kent and Lynn for several months, they considered him family as well.

"Amber will be in our prayers, you can be sure of that. Don't worry, Mom. Remember Casey had a similar problem last year, and he did just fine."

"I had forgotten that. Thanks, Lynn. Tell Courtney and Matthew I'll keep them posted."

Jill was equally comforting. When Kate called, Maureen and William were both home, and their vibrant voices cheered her considerably. Kate had just started a letter to her sister telling about Amber's problem, when Dr. Scheer called. Her first words were, "Amber's doing just fine."

"Thank God," breathed Kate.

"He's making a strong recovery. You've done a good job with him, Kate."

Kate smiled her appreciation for this compliment. "Well, I try."

With Amber's prognosis good, Kate could think of other things-- tomorrow's agenda for instance. She had promised several Sunday School students that they could come to the church after school for some set painting.

"It will be easier if we just do it ourselves," Martha had suggested when she heard Kate's plans.

"That's quite true," Kate had agreed. "But I've chosen kids that work well together, and I'll have everything set up ahead of time. What could go wrong?"

AMBER KNOWS BEST

Chapter Twenty-Three

Kate steadied herself on the open screened door as she reached for the unwieldy pole used to unhook the bird feeder. The light snow had changed to sleet overnight making the deck slippery and treacherous. She had forgotten to ask Kent to fill the bird feeder on his last visit, and the yellow grosbeaks had awakened her this morning, squabbling over the last remaining dregs of sunflower seeds and hulls.

Once, when Reed was still living, she had attempted to unlatch the bird feeder, but the weight of the nine foot pole, combined with the heavy feeder itself, was just too much. This morning Kate was determined to add "refilling the feeder" to the slowly growing list of items she could manage herself.

Slowly she swung the long pole toward the feeder and carefully positioned the nail at the pole's end into the round eye rod that connected the dome cover to the feeder itself. She hooked that to the one-inch metal hook on the underside of the extended two by four. Kate kept repeating, "I think I can, I think I can."

With strength she didn't know she possessed, Kate eased the bird feeder off the nail, and just started the wide arc swing back to the deck, when her arms began trembling and her foot slipped on the icy deck.

Kate watched in horror as the expensive feeder slipped off the pole and dropped fifteen feet to the ground below. "No!" her anguished cry sliced the air, emptying the nearby trees of all inhabitants.

Pole still in hand, Kate peered over the railing. From her aerial view the crash site looked grim. It appeared only a few sunflower seeds survived.

Getting to the area to further inspect the damage wasn't easy. The boardwalks hadn't been shoveled from the original snowfall, and now were sleet crusted and slippery. Kate guessed the feeder landed halfway down the hill near one of several small springs.

"I need to buy hip boots for this kind of operation," Kate muttered as she left the boardwalk area and plowed through the stalks of wild raspberry bushes poking through the snow. She reached the plastic dome first and discovered the snow had cushioned the fall, and it had survived. The main portion of the feeder, however, was not even in sight.

"I should have brought a shovel," Kate berated herself as she dug under the snow with her foot. She had about given up hope when she noticed a squirrel sitting on a rock beyond the spring, munching on a sunflower seed. As he pawed under the snow he uncovered the bottom part of the feeder. Kate slowly moved in that direction, carefully picking her way through the uneven ground. She stepped across the spring and brushed off the snow-packed container. Miraculously, it too appeared intact, but the bottom was stuck securely in the creek bed. Using her toe as a wedge, she partially dislodged the vessel, and straddling the creek, bent to pick it up. As Kate did so, she lost her equilibrium and fell backward, missing the icy water by inches. For a while Kate remained seated, torn between anger and tears. Then in resignation she lay back on the icy mattress, staring up at the now empty two-by-four jutting out like an index finger overhead.

"If there were only some way to swing the feeder closer to the deck," she mused. "But only a mechanical marvel could figure that one out."

Suddenly Kate sat upright. "That's it! Why didn't I think of it before?" This insight gave Kate renewed energy. She gathered together all the parts of the feeder, and cautiously made her way back to the house. Chilled to the bone by now, she ran the bath water and stayed submerged until her body began to thaw. It seemed strange to soak without Amber's presence. Watching Kate's bath proceedings was just another of her feline friend's quirks.

The sleet had stopped before Kate headed toward the church. She hoped the morning's debacle with the bird feeder wouldn't set the tone for the rest of the day. She reminded herself that some good might come from that near disaster. She would have to wait till tomorrow to look into that possibility.

"Good Afternoon, Kate." Pastor Southwick was sprinkling salt on the church entrance ramp. "Can I help you carry anything?"

"Sure." Kate indicated a box in her trunk. "There's paint in there, so it's a bit heavy. You can just set it on one of the tables in the basement." The major set piece of the Christmas musical was a time machine (a-la-refrigerator packing box), which was what the kids would be painting after school today.

"Where will the children be working?" Pastor Southwick questioned somewhat warily.

"As far from that area as we can." Kate indicated the carpet recently installed for the preschool/kindergarten class. The rug had been a gift from the Women's Society at Martha's request, and one of the reasons Martha had suggested that she and Kate do the set painting.

The drop cloths were in place, and the paint supplies ready, when the six volunteers arrived. Kate had expected only four.

"Kari and Lee Ann are staying over at my house tonight. Is it all right if they help, Mrs. Stenson?"

The girls Heather mentioned were strangers to Kate. She smiled at the newcomers. "I suppose that is OK, Molly. But I didn't bring extra shirts."

"Oh, we'll be careful," the new girls assured Kate. The boy volunteers, also sixth graders, were unusually quiet throughout this conversation, and the instructions that followed.

"I suggest you take turns, and two paint at a time. The boys paint the back and front portions, and the girls do the sides and the trim work." Kari whispered something to Heather and both giggled.

"Are there any questions?" Everybody shook their heads.

"Fine, I'm going upstairs to get the manger out of the supply closet," Kate said. "I'll be back soon."

Kate hadn't been in the supply closet in awhile. Actually, the term "supply" was a misnomer. That term inferred there were closets with other specialties. This closet, located just off the narthex, was the one and only closet this small church possessed. As such, it housed a multitude of unrelated items--all to be sorted through or climbed over before Kate reached the back shelves where the manger and various other Christmas paraphernalia were stacked.

Hanging wall banners were the first obstacles Kate encountered. The worship committee had placed them in the order of the church seasons, so she was careful not to jostle the rack they were hanging from.

The closet floor was an obstacle in itself, littered with the ends of brooms, shovels, ladders and easels. Kate stepped over and around and through the clutter until she reached the back shelves. A large box filled with Christmas tree lights and ornaments jutted from the first shelf, while the manger rested just out of Kate's reach above it.

"I hate being short," Kate grumbled, looking around for something to elevate her five foot two stature. She chose a child's wooden chair with a cracked seat that had been put in the closet for repair, and probably long since forgotten. The chair looked safe enough to Kate as she stepped up, steadying herself on the box of Christmas ornaments. She hadn't noticed the Christmas tree stand leaning against the manger. As Kate pulled the manger from the shelf, the tree stand came too. Its unexpected arrival caught Kate off balance. The chair tipped over, and so did Kate.

At that precise moment, Pastor Southwick appeared at the closet door with some news. "Mrs. Stenson, I thought you might like to know that several of your set painters just ran past my office with blue paint in their hair."

Chapter Twenty-Four

As soon as Kate arrived at the high school, she put on her sneakers and headed at a fast clip down the hall. The afternoon of set painting had taken much longer than planned, and she was late for her walking date.

"Hey, wait for me!" Martha called from the main entrance. Kate didn't think she'd ever hear those words from her friend. When they started their daily exercise program three months ago, Kate was the one constantly playing the game of "catch up," whether they were walking or cross country skiing. That was to be expected. After all, Martha was fifteen years younger than Kate. The differences didn't stop there. Martha was tall and slim – definitely a Type A personality. She, and her husband Ed, owned an insurance and real estate business in Lake Crystal, so she had a pleasant public persona to uphold. Martha walked the fastest on those days when her customers were impossibly rude or their requests were ridiculously unattainable.

"You ought to try what my friend Grace finally did," Kate suggested to Martha on one of their first walks together.

"Who is Grace? Do I know her?"

"Oh, no. This was back in the fifties when Reed and I were newly married and living in New York City. Grace and I were business representatives for the New York Telephone Company. It was during the Korean War, copper was in short supply, so you could only get new telephone service or single party service on an emergency basis. Most people had two party lines, and the complaints came in by the bushels. When the customers were mad as heck, they'd call their business 'reps' and give us both barrels. Sometimes I had to have Reed explain the names they called me. What was worse, after all that name calling, we were instructed to reply in our most dulcet tones: 'I'm sorry you feel that way, Mrs. Lenguinee. Let me see what I can do to help.'

"I was new on the job, but Grace had been listening to this garbage, and responding with this polite patter, for a year, and her marriage was beginning to suffer. After she got home from work, her husband, Fred, was the target of Grace's pent up feelings. If he complained about the least little thing, Grace would unleash her tongue and tell Fred everything she wanted to say to Mrs. Lenguinee.

"Grace and I were having lunch one day when she told me that Fred had suggested something to help her release those tensions BEFORE she got home. After work that same day, I was walking with Grace to the subway when suddenly she stopped dead still on the sidewalk, threw back her head, and shouted the 'S' word loud enough for all lower Manhattan to hear."

"My gosh," Martha giggled. "What happened? Did she stop traffic or what?"

"This is New York City we're talking about, Martha. The sidewalk crowd gave her a little wider berth for a few seconds, but then continued on without a backward glance. I, on the other hand, went into shock. This was so out of character and unexpected, I stepped off the curb into the path of an oncoming cab."

"Kate!" Martha gasped. "Were you hurt?"

"Not unless you consider being scared out of ten years growth being hurt. The cab driver swerved at the last second, gave me the finger, hollered 'get sober lady' and left me incoherent for the rest of the subway trip home. From then on Grace promised to vent her feelings AFTER she and I separated."

"Kate," Martha asked, "are you suggesting I try this form of tension release in Lake Crystal?"

Kate shrugged. "It worked for Grace."

"Forget it, Kate, I'll just walk it off."

That is just what Kate was trying to do this afternoon--walk it off. "Hey, Martha. I'll race you to the next exit sign."

Due to the icy road and ski trail conditions, Kate and Martha were walking the halls of Lake Crystal High School. Both preferred to exercise outside, but that was taboo today.

"I won," Kate declared with a grin. Then she noticed Martha staring at her hair.

"Are you making a fashion statement?"

"What?"

"Is that a streak of blue in your hair?"

Kate held up her matching blue fingernails. "I'm making a statement all right." Before Martha could question her further, Kate blurted out, "And if you dare say, 'I told you so,' you're dead!"

Picking up her walking pace, Kate quickly related the "painting the set" story up to the point where Pastor Southwick announced he had seen the set painters running past his office.

"What did you do?" Martha asked.

"I found the culprits in the bathrooms trying to wash out the evidence."

"Who started the paint fight?"

Kate snorted. "Martha, you're a mother. What kind of question is that? All I know is I was steaming by the time I reached the bathrooms. I had counted to ten only because Pastor Southwick was within hearing range. A war of words was probably what those kids were expecting. It wasn't what they got. Instead, I asked them to sit down around the table in the adult classroom. Then I went downstairs and brought up the lemonade and cookies I had previously prepared for their treat."

Martha chuckled, "I bet the kids weren't expecting that after what they had just done."

"I gather not. From the time I told them to sit down, until after we ate our treat, there was nothing but uncomfortable silence, and occasional nervous glances from one kid to the other. When the snack was over, I explained in carefully measured tones, that I wasn't interested in how the paint war had started. I was only interested in the damage that had been done.

"With all six kids in tow, we surveyed the formerly white bathroom walls, and the formerly gray linoleum floor that extended beyond the drop cloths. Fortunately, the multi-flecked carpeting in the preschool area was far enough away from the war zone to be spared the paint fallout. Without any back talk or any further conversation, the group spent the next hour on their knees--and I don't mean in prayer."

"Did the paint all come out?"

"Actually, except for some white paint touch-up need in the bathrooms--which I will do--the basement and bathroom floors have never looked cleaner."

"How about the time machine?"

"They finished that, too. Took turns doing it one at a time. That was their idea." Martha shook her head.

"And," continued Kate, "What is even more amazing, after everything was all cleaned up, each helper apologized to Pastor Southwick for their behavior, and Heather's friends asked if they could come to church school next Sunday."

"Go figure," Martha shrugged.

* * *

Later that evening, as Kate sipped coffee from her mug inscribed, "Home is Where the Cat Is", she reviewed the day's disastrous events. Here she was, home alone, without even her beloved Amber to listen to her woes, and yet she felt strangely "up beat." The bird feeder parts still lay on the island counter, so she decided to clean up the pieces before she tried the reassembling. As she scrubbed, she thought, "Why wait till tomorrow? I'll call him now."

On the second ring, a jovial voice chirped, "Clifford here, who's there?"

"Kate Stenson here, Cliff, and I've got a problem."

"Big or little?"

"You know no problem is too big for Cliff Kelly," Kate teased. "Could you possibly fit me into your work schedule tomorrow some time?"

"Sure thing, Kate. Do I need to bring any special equipment?"

"It's the outside birdfeeder, Cliff. I want you to figure out a way I can swing it closer to the deck for refilling."

"Oh, yeah. I remember that son-of-a-gun. I can stop by about 7:45. Too early?"

"Just right."

After she hung up, she thought about the feeder problem. Then she got out some paper and began putting down some ideas of her own.

The bed sheets seemed unusually cold to Kate as she crawled into her side of the antique four-poster. The bed seemed so big now. Funny, she thought, Reed hadn't shared her bed for over a year, but she still slept on 'her" side--leaving space for--what? Even Amber rarely occupied the area vacated by his master.

Kate used to kid Reed that she'd kept him around all those years because he was cheaper than an electric blanket. Kate plumped up her pillow, turned over in the other direction, and warmed up with thoughts of Dr. Paul Dubois.

AMBER KNOWS BEST

Chapter Twenty-Five

Kate raised her head from the pillow and squinted at the clock on the dresser. The alarm was set for seven, and when she saw it was only 6:30, she flopped back on her pillow and relaxed, glad to have some time to make sense of the dream she had just had.

Kate was no stranger to the world of dreams. For most of her life, dreams were a nightly event.

"I never dream," Reed declared during one of their premarital conversations years ago.

"Everybody dreams, "Kate insisted. "You just don't remember yours. You're lucky!"

Kate rationalized that dreaming was just another manifestation of her many phobias. As a child, Kate was afraid of the dark, and it made bedtime a particular trial. By the time she reached grade school, Kate had worked out a routine to lessen her anxiety somewhat. In those early years, Kate's family lived in a two-story house with three bedrooms and a bath upstairs. As the youngest child, she was the first to retire. To assure herself that her bedroom was uninhabited by nocturnal phantoms, she performed a ritual every night before retiring. She would flip on wall switches as she ran up the backstairs, through the hallway, and into her bedroom. The large walk-in clothes closet that she and her sister shared, was her first concern. She'd swing open the closet door and then hide behind it, lest some evil creature jump out and overpower her. When that didn't happen, she would step inside, pull the ceiling light cord, and check in, around, and under the hanging clothes for any suspicious looking lumps or foreign objects.

When the closet passed her inspection, Kate would shut the door securely and look under the twin beds. She had the twin bed closest to the hallway, having convinced her sister that her bed next to the window had the advantage of cool breezes during the hot Indiana summer nights.

The real reason was quite different. When Kate got up to go to the bathroom, she couldn't be sure some foot-grabbing fiends hadn't slipped underneath the bed while she was down the hall. To avoid those multi-handed creatures, Kate would stand in the hallway and jump sometimes many feet onto the bed. In fifth grade she held the record for standing broad jump, probably because of all that nighttime practice.

Despite all these precautions, Kate's dreams continued and sometimes turned ugly.

"I sometimes have nightmares," Kate warned Reed.

"Nightmares?" Reed asked. "What sort of nightmares?"

"Actually it's the same nightmare that I've been having since I was in grade school. I'm only half awake when it happens, but I should warn you, I get loud and violent." Kate smiled and raised her eyebrows. "Still want to marry me?"

"I don't know? Tell me more."

"I'm a light sleeper. Something, probably a noise, disturbs my sleep, and as I open my eyes I see a dark figure standing close, ready to grab me. I scream bloody murder, and do whatever it takes to get away from the 'the evil one' I call him."

Reed shook his head. "Sounds pretty unnerving for anyone sleeping in the vicinity."

"You're so right! The first time I had this nightmare, I ran into my parent's bedroom, screaming at the top of my lungs."

"What did your parents do?"

"Both sat bolt upright, and the hair on their heads literally stood on end."

"You're lucky you are still alive."

"That's not all. I pulled this stunt once in the Tri Delta dorm during finals week."

"What did the gals think of that?"

"They told me, if it had happened during pledge week, I wouldn't have made the sorority.

Kate never told Reed about her other, less disturbing dreams. In those dreams Kate was forever in a quandary. She was the student without the right textbook, the teacher without a lesson plan, the secretary with no knowledge of shorthand. Kate knew it wouldn't take a dream expert to explain those feelings of helplessness and inadequacy.

Kate fluffed up her pillow and watched the rose tint of dawn reflecting off the glass covering the pastel peony still life she had drawn for her parents years ago. She couldn't so easily analyze the dream she had had last night. For once it wasn't a nightmare--or even a particularly disturbing dream--although there were aspects of both. The mysterious figure was there, but he was neither dark nor forbidding. He had an almost familiar essence urging Kate to join him. He reached for Kate's hands and pulled her closer. The warmth and pressure of his touch was sensual and Kate wanted to move to him, but something stopped her. It was then that she woke up.

The alarm prompted Kate to roll out of her warm bed and prepare for Cliff Kelly's visit. Certainly there was nothing mysterious about Cliff. He was as open and honest and likeable as they come.

Call it Providence (Kate's choice) or call it Fool's Luck, the Kelly's and Stemson's paths were bound to cross. About the same time Kate and Reed happened on to their vacation dream cabin on Lake Crystal, Cliff Kelly and his wife, Myrna, were checking with a United Farm Agency in northern Wisconsin for a vacation hide-a-way of their own.

After high school, Cliff started out working the family farm in northern Illinois. He would have stayed there, too, if his uncle hadn't begged him to come to Indiana and help him build barns. That's where he met Myrna. He not only got a new career, he got a wife. Cliff was not only good at building barns; he was good at building houses, and anything else anyone needed.

By the time he turned forty, Cliff had more work than he needed, and when Myrna talked him into looking for vacation property, she didn't have to talk very hard. Cliff liked to hunt, and Myrna liked to fish. The first property they were shown was an abandoned farm two miles west of Lake Crystal. As they drove into the yard, an eight-point buck was standing beside the old barn. Cliff told Myrna he'd see to it that she got to fish whenever she liked, but this was the property they were going to buy.

By the time Cliff and Myrna moved to Lake Crystal full time, everyone in town knew about Kelly's talents. When a new cook was needed at the high school, Myrna applied and got the job. Whenever anybody had a building job that needed an expert craftsman, Cliff got a call.

It was Cliff who had figured out how to extend the bird feeder and fool the squirrels. The year before Reed died, Cliff was often at the Stenson's for one reason or another. Over the years Reed and Cliff had become good friends, and as Reed grew weaker, Cliff's visits were a tonic for Kate as well.

She had hot coffee and blueberry muffins ready when Cliff arrived promptly at seven forty-five. His clear blue eyes twinkled as he handed Kate a paper bag. "Here's something to add to your toy shelf."

Cliff was a toy maker. His garage served as a workshop where he mass-produced all his designs. "It satisfies the child within all of us," was Cliff's answer to why he made the toys.

"This one's for the birds," Cliff chuckled as he watched Kate pull out a facsimile of a Redheaded Woodpecker. He gave the bird a tap on its red head, and it pecked its way down a wire tree, never stopping until it reached bottom.

"I love it," Kate squealed. "At last something for the grandchildren that doesn't need batteries."

As Cliff buttered his muffins, Kate moved to her desk, got a piece of graph paper on which she'd made some drawings, and laid it on the table by Cliff's coffee mug. "I know you've toys to make, Santa, so I won't take up too much of your time. Do you recognize that contraption?"

"I sure do. That's the hard-to-retrieve bird feeder. But it looks like you've made it retrievable. Is that a big hinge you've added?"

"I think I remember seeing a hinge that size on your old barn door. Do they still make them Cliff?"

"I know where I can find one. I see you've also added a pull chain and a removable rod to keep the hinge from swinging, except for refilling." He turned and smiled. "Say, Kate, do you have a patent for this?"

"Necessity's the mother of invention, Cliff, along with--," Kate was searching for another word--a word she'd never used before in connection with herself.

"I'll get at it today, Kate. In the meantime, I'll fill the bird feeder for you. When it comes time to fill it again, you'll be able to do it yourself."

That's it, thought Kate. I'll be able to do it myself! Sweet independence.

Chapter Twenty-Six

Boots, Blackie, and Twin materialized the minute Cliff's truck disappeared from view. Kate let them in the warm entrance room. Reed had started this practice when the temperature dipped below freezing. "The kids need a warm breakfast," he'd insisted. Then he would sit on a small chair he'd taken out for that purpose, and talk to the cats as they ate.

It was awhile after Reed's death before the Outsiders fully accepted her. They kept expecting Reed's return. Kate felt the tears come again as she thought about those months of explaining. "He's not coming back, kitties, so you're going to have to take me as a poor substitute."

Little Twin had been the hardest to convince, and she was reluctant to come in today, even though there was snow in the air, and ice beginning to form in the cove.

Blackie came first, followed by Boots and Twin. Kate marveled once again at the differences in appearance and personalities of these siblings. As she stroked the wild ones, she longed for the silky feel of Amber's thick coat and was suddenly apprehensive. Dr. Scheer had said she would call Kate if there were problems, but…. The phone interrupted her thoughts and hurried her inside. "Maybe that's her calling now," Kate picked up the receiver with a sense of anxiety.

"Kate, this is Paul."

Kate was caught off guard. She was prepared to talk to Dr. Joanne Scheer, not Dr. Paul Dubois.

Paul filled the silence. "I'm trying to reach the Kate Stenson residence."

"And you have." Now Kate was embarrassed. "I'm sorry, Paul, I was expecting someone else --Dr. Scheer."

"Is there something wrong, Kate?"

"No. I mean…" Doggone it thought Kate, my mother and doctors! They can always tell when I'm lying.

"Excuse me, Paul." She put down the phone and reached in her jeans pocket for a Kleenex. She also tried to retrieve the confident, independent woman she thought she'd become.

"I'm back," she sniffed.

"Do you have a cold, Kate? Your voice sounds a little different..." Without waiting for Kate's answer, Paul continued on, explaining the reason for his early morning call. "I could not sleep last night. I had this uneasy feeling that you were in some sort of trouble. I know I was probably foolish to..." He seemed to be searching for the right words and Kate wondered if it was difficult for a man of science to admit acting on hunches.

"Paul, you were right. There is something wrong here, but not with me. It's Amber. Dr. Scheer is our vet. I am expecting a call from her."

"I'm sorry to hear that. What happened to Amber?"

"Two days ago I came home to find him in excruciating pain. Luckily, Dr. Scheer got here quickly and diagnosed bladder stones. She took him to her clinic and operated the same day. I know Amber is in good hands, and I shouldn't even be concerned, but..."

"But he's an important member of your family." Paul's deep voice was soft with compassion, "And of course you miss him. When does Dr. Scheer say Amber can come home?"

"It depends how soon he starts back on solid food. Amber has always been a finicky eater, Paul." Kate sighed, "And now he'll have to be on a special diet."

"Kate, it has been my experience with pets and with people," Paul was using his encouraging doctor tone now, "that we know what's good for us. You can be sure that Amber wants to come home as much as you want him there. Somehow Dr. Scheer will communicate that message, and Amber will do what it takes to get home soon."

"Thanks. I needed to hear that – and Paul," Kate's voice was almost a whisper. "I was thinking of you last night too." This time the pause that followed did not need filling.

Paul's predictions were on target. Dr. Scheer called only minutes after Paul and Kate's conversation, reporting that even she was amazed at Amber's quick recovery. He was eating solid food with apparent relish and should be ready for release from the clinic the following afternoon.

That timing was just right for Kate. The storytelling workshop was schedule from nine to one. For once Kate didn't need more time to get organized; instead, she managed a "same day" appointment at Vera's for a haircut, shampoo and blow dry. On her way home she noticed the bookmobile parked by the Village Hall and picked up some light reading, which included a reread of "The Greatest Christmas Pageant Ever."

The snow had picked up intensity a bit, so she stoked up the wood stove and put a Lean Cuisine TV dinner in the oven for supper. It had been awhile since she had written her friend Kerrie, so she took the time now to bring her up to date. She didn't mention her correspondence and phone conversations with Paul Dubois. After all, Kate rationalized, she and Paul were just good friends. Besides, she was an independent woman now, and independent women get along quite well alone--don't they?

AMBER KNOWS BEST

Chapter Twenty-Seven

Kate woke up to the scraping of a snowplow and pleasant thoughts of her reunion with Amber. She judged the time to be about 6:30 by the soft blue gray light outside her bedroom windows. More snow had been predicted and she guessed that was what the plow was about. The wide expanse of front room windows framed a winter scene. Snow mounded each tree limb and highlighted the northeast side of their trunks. Kate thought she might start a Christmas card pencil sketch had she more time.

The bird feeder dome had a lopsided cap of snow, Kate noticed as she sipped her coffee. The next filling, Kate smiled, she could do herself.

This new confidence spilled over in her thoughts about her leadership activities for the teacher workshop today. The one variable she couldn't control was how well the teachers attending today's meeting would respond to the work she had planned for them.

She needn't have worried. Gail Shannon had been told about Amber's illness through Kate's granddaughter, Courtney, and scheduled Kate's part of the workshop accordingly. Several teachers made a point of catching Kate with positive comments before she left the building. One said, "I never thought I could tell stories until I saw how well those youngsters in Gail's class did it…"

"Yes," echoed another. "When it came our turns, it was hard to refuse."

"You proved you could do it beautifully," Kate smiled, waved and was gone.

In mid-November, daylight is at a premium in northern Wisconsin. Kate knew she would have to hustle to make Dr. Scheer's rural clinic and be home before dark. The doctor had Amber in the Pet Taxi and ready when Kate arrived. Although it wasn't safe veterinary practice, according to Dr. Scheer, nevertheless she allowed Kate to put the Taxi in the passenger seat next to her for their ride home.

The trip to Lake Crystal was full of conversation, albeit a mite one-sided. Kate told Amber how she had missed him, what she had done while he was away, and her plans for the upcoming holiday.

"I had planned to spend Thanksgiving with Jill and the kids." Amber lifted his head. "Of course that was before you got sick. Kent and Lynn always have Thanksgiving with Lynn's folks, so you and I will keep each other company."

Amber dozed off the first half hour of the trip and didn't wake up till Kate set the Taxi down in the front room. Dr. Scheer hadn't fed Amber, knowing the car ride might make him nauseous. So the first thing Kate did was fill Amber's dish with the new diet cat food. Amber was starved for both food and affection. Kate sat on a low stool beside him and stroked Amber as he ate. They were a couple of happy campers. When the phone rang later that evening, Kate knew who it would be.

"It's Paul, Kate. How is Amber?"

Paul's deep voice gave Kate's pulse a jump-start. "I brought him home this afternoon, and he hasn't stopped purring since he got inside. Would you like to hear?"

Kate put the receiver next to Amber who was curled up on a nearby dining room chair. Amber rubbed his chin against the mouthpiece. "You just got rubbed Paul. Whatever you said must have pleased him."

"I told him to take good care of you, Kate."

"He hasn't left my side since we got home. I'm going to find it difficult leaving him when I go to church tomorrow."

"He'll be fine, Kate. How's the weather in Lake Crystal? Have you had any more snow?"

"It snows some every day, enough to keep everything white. The lake is still partially open, but it won't be for long. How are Ann and the kids?"

"We're getting together at Thanksgiving. I'm going to Minneapolis for the week. In fact, that is another reason I'm calling. Kate, Ann asked me to invite you to have Thanksgiving at her home, if you haven't made plans already."

Kate didn't respond immediately because her mind was so full of conflicting emotions. Her heart raced wildly. One side of her wanted to gush, "I'd love to go to Minneapolis with you Paul, or anywhere else you might want to go. Getting to know you better is right at the top of my list of things I want to do."

Her other side, the new in-control, independent side, reminded her: Of course you can't leave Lake Crystal for Thanksgiving in Minneapolis. How could you possibly explain that rash decision to Jill and Kent? Jill is already suspicious of Paul's motive. Besides, you would be falling right back into that dependency pattern you've been trying to overcome.

In the end, she steered a middle course.

"Paul, that certainly is nice of Ann to think of me, but I don't want to leave Amber just yet. Jill has invited me to come to Middleton for Thanksgiving, but I plan to tell her I won't be able to make it."

"Ann's husband has a private plane, Kate. We could be at Skyport mid-morning and bring you back early evening."

Paul wasn't making it easy for Kate. She felt herself flush. It was like saying "no" to her old passion, Snickers candy bars; the temptation to give in was that strong

" I would like that, but…" Be honest, Kate, her conscience prompted. "Paul, the truth is I haven't said much to either Jill or Kent about you."

"Why is that, Kate?"

"I'm not entirely sure. It's a side of me you haven't seen perhaps. I've always had a difficult time with decisions. I'm working on it."

"Is there anything I can do to change your mind?"

"NO Paul!" Even Kate was surprised by the force of her response. She felt the tears start and mopped them with her hand.

When she said nothing further, Paul spoke. "I understand, Kate. It is important to stay with family members when they are sick." Paul's voice was hoarse. Kate worried now that she might be dredging up painful memories for Paul, memories of his wife's last hours when he wasn't with her. This was certainly not what Kate had intended.

But the damage was done, intended or not, and the rest of their conversation was inconsequential. Kate asked for and received Ann's address and telephone number, planning to write and thank her for the holiday invitation. As difficult as the decision had been to make, Kate felt she had been right to turn down Paul's invitation. Yet, she also realized now just how much she looked forward to Paul's calls and letters, and knew her strong refusal might well have put an end to all that.

After church Sunday, when Kate called Middleton to cancel her visit, Jill said her children would have been inconsolable had they not had cats of their own that had been to the animal hospital recently. The two females, Kissifer and Andrea, had just been spayed. Sassy, the male would be neutered in a month or two.

"Where is Amber, Gramma?" Maureen wanted to know during her allotted time on this phone visit.

"He's on the blue antique bonnet box by the front windows, Maureen, watching your cousins Courtney and Matthew sliding on the south hill."

"Daddy is going to take us sliding on our back hill after our naps today."

"The hill that has the big curve near the bottom where you have the tree fort?"

"Uh huh."

"Maureen, ask you Mother to take the camcorder along so I can see your sliding fun when you come visit me at Christmas time."

When it was William's turn, Kate asked him where the cats were.

"Sleeping on top of each other in Daddy's recliner. Do you know what Sassy did yesterday, Gramma? He went swimming."

"He did?" Kate laughed, convinced that Matthew's three-year-old imagination was working overtime. That was not the case she discovered when Jill took over the conversation.

"Yes, Sassy was swimming, Mother. We knew Sass liked water when he kept jumping in the shower with Keith every morning. But yesterday was something else again. Matthew wanted to take a bubble bath. While we were filling the tub, Matthew and I left the bathroom just long enough to make a clothes selection. When we returned, there was Sassy."

"In the water?"

"You bet. All we could see was Sass's black head above the bubbles, swimming around the edge of the tub, just as happy as a – seal."

"That's a good one. Amber likes to jump in the tub after I've emptied my bath water, but he's never joined me. Next time take a picture of Sassy doing bubble laps. I'd like one for my pet scrapbook."

* * *

Later, before Kate took her turn sliding down the hill, she told Matthew and Courtney about Sassy's swimming skills. When she rolled off the toboggan, just before reaching the creek, Courtney screamed, "Who's going swimming now, Gramma?"

After that exciting escape, the rest of the days before Thanksgiving seemed dull and just a little depressing. Kate dutifully wrote Paul's daughter, Ann, thanking her for the invitation. Cliff installed the retrievable hanging bird feeder using Kate's design. Amber was obviously feeling better by the day. All reasons for Kate to feel good. Yet something was missing. Thanksgiving eve, Kate got out the journal she had started three months ago at Dr. Gessler's insistence. Perhaps here she would find the answer.

Chapter Twenty-Eight

Kate had forgotten just how much walking helped revive her. By the time she got back home, she still wasn't quite ready to leave the outdoor splendor. The fresh snow on the side hill was so inviting, Kate went inside only long enough to drop off her mail and milk, then grabbed the plastic toboggan from the garage on her way back out.

As she studied the course from the top of the hill, Kate could still faintly see her original run. One factor she failed to consider was the low temperature, which increased her speed. She also failed to remember, until too late, that the course she traveled on last led directly to the creek.

After a strong push off, the toboggan picked up speed, then hit a snowdrift. For several exhilarating seconds, Kate and toboggan were airborne, but when they made snow contact again they were within feet of the creek.

"No!" Kate shrieked, as she came to a watery stop.

Almost immediately her expletive was answered. "Hold on! I'm on my way!"

Kate didn't have to turn around. She recognized the voice. The icy water inched up her back. She was certainly in no physical danger, but her dignity was demolished. The more she moved to extricate herself, the faster the cold spring water filled the toboggan, her boots, and her ski pants.

Unceremoniously, her rescuer grabbed under her arms and pulled her back up the creek bank until she could stand up. Kate knew she had to turn around eventually, but delayed it as long as she could. When the rescuer and the rescuee finally made eye contact, the reaction was simultaneous. Although both tried, neither could contain their feelings. Kate and Paul stood knee deep in the snow, threw back their heads and laughed like idiots.

Paul regained his composure first. "I'm sorry Kate. You must be verging on hypothermia about now. Let me help you into the house."

Kate's first move was to get her toboggan out of the creek, and then she let Paul take her hand and pull her waterlogged body up the hill. There was a four-wheel drive parked by the garage. Paul broke the silence, "Have you had lunch? I tried to reach you earlier. I was hoping we could go to Skyport."

By now they had reached the warm entrance room, and Kate sat on a bench to remove her boots. As she turned them upside down by the electric heat fan, water dribbled on the carpeted floor.

"No Paul, I haven't had lunch. But I won't be going anywhere till my boots dry out." Paul's face reflected his disappointment. "However, if you are willing to wait while I take a quick bath, we can have lunch here. I've got some pizza in the freezer."

Kate couldn't believe she said that, but she wasn't sorry. It was a decision she wouldn't have made twenty-four hours ago. In response, Paul flashed a smile that generated a quick start to Kate's warming process.

Once inside, Kate started to tend the wood stove, but Paul had other ideas. "Let me do that, Kate. The sooner you get out of those wet clothes, the better."

Kate had to agree. In fact, the hot bath felt so good to her cold bones, she soaked longer than she intended. She quickly slipped on the warmest outfit she could find--a teal sweat suit she had purchased during her visit with Jill. Kate noticed she still had hip room in a size 12 these days.

Paul was sitting on the couch and didn't see Kate at first. His attention was focused on a large white cat sniffing his pants legs. Slowly Paul bent over and let the cat sniff his outstretched hand, all the while speaking words of encouragement in a soft voice.

Kate watched in silent fascination. Since Reed's death, Amber had never approached strangers without Kate's encouragement. First Amber accepted Paul's petting, then when Paul straightened up and leaned back against the couch, Amber jumped up into Paul's lap. At this point Paul noticed Kate, and smiled as he petted his new friend.

"This is Amber, I presume. Ann told me about him. She was right. If I didn't know better I'd think it was my old cat, Casanova, reincarnated. Oh, by the way, Kate. You got two telephone calls while you were bathing."

Kate looked surprised and Paul looked a bit sheepish. "I don't know what possessed me to answer the phone. I think I took both of your callers by surprise. The first caller was your daughter Jill, and the second caller was Kerrie, I believe."

Kate grimaced and shook her head, "Oh, oh."

"I'm sorry Kate. What kind of problems did I cause?"

"I'm sure the damage isn't irreparable. Did either leave a message?"

"Your daughter was sure she had dialed the wrong number, and I'm not entirely certain she believed me even after I assured her this was the Stenson residence. I gather Paul Dubois was not a name that she recognized."

"She must have forgotten," Kate replied. "When I received your letter in Middleton, I explained that you are my new neighbor. I'll call her back as soon as I get the salad made and start the pizza. What did Kerrie have to say?"

"From Kerrie's response I assumed she had heard about me."

Kate laughed. "Why? What gave you that impression?"

"After I gave her my name she said to tell you, 'obviously the molehill has become a mountain,' and then she hung up."

"Skyport can't hold a candle to this view."

Paul was standing near the windows drinking coffee while Kate poured hot fudge sauce over a generous scooping of vanilla ice cream, finishing it off with a dollop of whipped topping. She put the dessert on the table and joined Paul at the windows.

"The folks next door have a real nice looking spread, don't you think?" Paul smiled and rested his hand on Kate's shoulder – near her neck. His touch sent shivers through her body.

Paul looked concerned, "Are you still cold?"

Kate started toward the table. "Not the best kind of weather for ice cream, but we'd better eat it before it melts."

Paul held Kate's chair for her, and she smiled her thanks.

"For a country boy, you've got wonderful manners."

"My Mom's influence. She wasn't raised on a farm like Dad. Her family moved to Hinsdale from the east. Her Dad, my grandfather, was a doctor."

Paul's voice softened when he spoke of his mother. Kate sensed there was a strong bond between Mother and son and difficult for Paul to talk about. She changed the subject.

"What brought you back to Lake Crystal so soon? I didn't expect you till the holidays."

"Jerry Walker called and told me I'd better get back up here before things got too deep."

"What do you think of the snow?"

"It's beautiful. I love it. I'm lucky the Hellman's prepared me for winter."

"What do you mean?"

"They left their tractor, snow plow, snow blower, and even a couple of snow machines. When I got here several days ago, I parked on the road outside the gate and walked in. It took me a half hour of snow blowing to get the tractor out and plowing," Paul spoke with genuine enthusiasm as he related his experience.

"You know, Paul, most of the summer people wouldn't share your joy in snow removal. They head south even before the leaves turn."

"I may not be one of those summer people for long. What would you think about having me as a full time neighbor?" Kate's heart caught in her throat.

"That's one of the things I did while I was back in Hinsdale. I put my house up for sale."

Kate hoped her feelings weren't too obvious. "That must have been a hard decision. What does Ann think about all this?"

"Oh, she's delighted. Ann has been urging, actually badgering me to do this for a year now. Once I stopped practicing medicine I haven't spent much time in the Hinsdale place. Too big and too many memories." Paul's voice broke, and Kate wanted to touch his hand resting close to hers on the table. She didn't, not trusting her own emotions.

"I've spent this past year traveling around. When I wasn't staying with Ann and the grandkids, I've been visiting friends like the Walkers."

Paul turned toward Kate and studied her face quietly.

"Kate, I've thought quite a bit about our last meeting, and what you said about Providence. Since Sue's death, I've been in hell." Paul stopped speaking and closed his eyes.

This time Kate put her hand over his. Her voice was little more than a whisper.

"I know Paul. Ann told me."

"Kate, I hated God for allowing Sue's death, but most of all I hated myself for not being with her as I promised I would be." Paul's eyes moved to the end table by the couch. A Bible was open to the scripture Kate had been reading earlier this morning.

"Shortly after the funeral, my pal, Jerry, sent me a book called 'Forgive and Forget.' I knew he meant well, but I couldn't read it. I didn't deserve to be forgiven.

"When I went back to Hinsdale this last time, I was looking over all the books I would need to pack when I moved, and I came across Jerry's gift. For some reason, I felt the need to read it, along with the Bible passages it suggested. After Mom's death I got turned off of religion, but Jerry never stopped helping through the rough spots in my life. He thought about becoming a minister before he turned to medicine. Now I'm beginning to see what he has that I've been missing."

Paul sighed. "Forgiving others is a lot easier than forgiving yourself. But I'm working on it, Kate. I'm working on it."

Paul appeared drained by his confession. The flame was burning low in the wood stove and he got up wearily, adding more logs to the fire. Amber jumped down from the couch, then jumped up on the wooden bench in front of the stove. Paul reached over to the cat and scratched his head.

"Amber. How are ya doin'? I'd forgotten how much company a cat can be."

Kate started clearing the table. "I don't think I could have survived this last year without one, or I guess I should say six cats, to talk to." Paul's chuckle lightened the mood.

"Let me help you 'ret up' the dishes." Kate smiled at his use of an old Hoosier expression.

"Thanks Paul, but there's not room between the counters for both of us."

"I think there is, Kate. You are looking very slim and svelte these days." Kate blushed under his close inspection. As he started around the counter, Kate pointed to the tape deck on the corner shelf by the window.

"Why don't you pick out a tape, while I stash these in the dishwasher?"

She was just putting in the last dish when the strains of the Glenn Miller orchestra playing "Moonlight Serenade" filled the room.

Paul tapped her on the shoulder, "May I have this dance, Madame?"

He didn't wait for an answer, but put his arm around her waist and pulled her close. Kate hadn't danced since high school. Reed had two left feet and didn't really hear the beat. Paul, on the other hand, moved with ease to the music. Neither said anything as they moved to the danceable rhythms of the old classics: "Unforgettable," "Serenade in Blue," and "Stardust."

When the music stopped, Kate said, "Where did you learn to dance so well?"

"Sue loved to dance. We belonged to a dance club. And you, my dear?"

"The last time I danced was my high school Senior Prom," Kate's eyes sparkled. "I'd forgotten how much I love it. Do you fast dance? I think 'Perfidia' is somewhere on the other side?"

Paul tightened his grip on his energized partner. "Whoa there, Kate. I'll answer your question if you promise to answer one I asked you a while back. Fair enough?"

"Fair enough." She quipped.

"No. I do not fast dance. BUT with the right instructor I might be willing to learn. OK?" Paul smiled.

Kate returned his smile and shook her head, "OK."

"Now it's your turn. Do you remember the question I asked?" Kate looked puzzled.

"What would you think of me as a full time neighbor?" Paul added, "I gather your friend Kerrie would not like that."

At the mention of Kerrie's name, Kate stiffened. "It doesn't matter what Kerrie thinks. I've also learned something about myself since the last time we were together." For a moment Kate questioned whether to go on. Then she relaxed, choosing her words with care. "Paul, most of my life I've done what other people wanted or expected me to do. That is, until Reed died. From that time on I've had to do things on my own, and believe me it hasn't been easy. I didn't even know how to handle a checkbook. Math was never my long suit."

Paul moved his hands down Kate's arms and squeezed her hands. "I'm sorry, Kate."

She resented the sympathy. "Don't be, Paul. I'm finding out for the first time I can do things on my own, and it's a good feeling."

Kate looked steadily in his eyes. "From now on I don't plan to be hurried. I'll make my decisions slowly, with careful consideration, and with God's help they'll be the right ones." Paul looked surprised. This obviously wasn't the reaction he expected.

Kate continued. "But, I still haven't answered your question, have I?"

"Maybe this isn't the best time to ask it."

Kate ignored his comment. "What should Kate Stenson think about having Paul Dubois as a full time neighbor? Let's see. So far he has found one of her favorite cats, removed a painful fishhook from her finger at no charge, and saved her from drowning in an icy creek. I'd say that's pretty good for starters."

Kate walked quickly to the tape deck, flipped on the fast forward button till she found the song she wanted to hear, and returned to Paul. "And he's one heck of a dancer."

Fastening her hands around his neck, she smiled. "This is one of my favorites – see what you think." Kate and Paul swayed to the music while the vocalist asked the question.

"Why do robins sing in December, long before the springtime is due? And even though its snowing, violets are growing. I know why and so do you.

"Why do breezes sigh every evening, whispering your name as they do? And why have I the feeling stars are on my ceiling? I know why, and so do you."

Paul smiled and started to speak. Kate put her finger on his lips. "Shh! I want to hear the words."

This time, still looking at Paul, Kate mouthed the words softly along with the vocalist. "When you smile at me, I hear gypsy violins. When you dance with me, I'm in heaven when the music begins.

"I can see the sun when it's raining, hiding every cloud from my view. And why do I see rainbows when I'm in your arms?"

This time Paul put his hand on Kate's lips while he said the words, "I know why, and so do you."

Kate didn't resist when Paul bent down and kissed her. The gentle warmth of his embrace told her he understood, and would respect her newfound independence. Together they would work through the steps of friendship, and perhaps, if it be God's will, even beyond.

The unmistakable sound of a cat's meow interrupted the moment. Both Kate and Paul turned to see Amber watching them like a chaperone at a school dance.

"I've got one last question that needs to be answered, Kate. Do you think cats can smile?"

Kate chuckled, "I think Amber just gave approval of your move. And from my point of view, Amber knows best."

AMBER KNOWS BEST

Made in the USA
Charleston, SC
29 October 2015